The Bill 5

By the same author
available from Thames Mandarin

The Bill
The Bill 2
The Bill 3
The Bill 4

The Bill 5

JOHN BURKE

Thames Mandarin

A Thames Mandarin Paperback

THE BILL 5

First published in Great Britain 1991
by Mandarin Paperbacks
Michelin House, 81 Fulham Road, London SW3 6RB
in association with
Thames Television International Limited
149 Tottenham Court Road, London W1P 9LL

Mandarin is an imprint of the Octopus Publishing Group

A CIP catalogue record for this title
is available from the British Library

ISBN 0 7493 0842 7

Printed and bound in Great Britain
by Cox & Wyman Ltd, Reading, Berks.

One

Viv Martella had at first regarded her transfer to CID as a promising step up the promotional ladder. No longer in impersonal uniform just like any other woman police constable, she could choose smart clothes, win the respect of authorities and the public on a quite different social level, and contribute any number of subtleties and shrewd perceptions to the investigations in which she would immediately be involved. That, at any rate, was how she had believed it would work out. Instead, here she was, pecking away at a typewriter while Tosh Lines and Jimmy Carver munched their lunchtime sandwiches; and any minute now, she sensed, someone would ask her to make a cup of coffee. After a week in the job she was beginning to wonder whether work as a secretarial temp, with a sideline in making tea, would not have been just as thrilling but with a much larger salary.

Detective Inspector Burnside emerged from his office and surveyed the scene without relish.

'What's going on here? I've seen more life in a bunch of Care Bears.'

'It's lunchtime, guv,' Lines pointed out, his voice muffled by a wayward crumb. 'I'll do Pearce in a sec.'

'Anybody heard how the Rosebery Park case is going?'

Martella tried to concentrate on her typing and not listen to this. Her life on the beat had never quite hardened her to some of the more gruesome aspects of policing, and this present inquiry was one she was glad not to be involved in. The murder squad were still trying to assemble a recognizable torso from bits which seemed to have been scattered over a wide area. The feet had turned up in a Sainsbury's bag by the

5

canal – well past the sell-by date, according to this morning's lurid report – but the hands were still missing.

Burnside nodded to Carver. 'Nip down there this afternoon and see how they're getting on. Have a snoop.' He glanced across at Martella, as if not wanting to leave her out. 'Make us a cup of coffee, will you, Viv.'

Carver brightened up 'Oh, Viv, if you're boiling the kettle . . .'

Her answer was lost in the screech of Tosh Lines pushing his chair back. Gulping down the last mouthful of sandwich, he headed downstairs to the interview room to question the suspect in good time before the mandatory custody review. A fascinating challenge, thought Martella grimly as she made two cups of coffee and came back to slam one down in the CID office, one on Burnside's desk.

The DI did not trouble to look up. 'Ta. And could you file that lot for me?' He waved abstractedly at a teetering pile of papers on the corner of his desk.

She gathered them up in her arms and was on her way out as DC Dashwood strode in, stony-faced. It looked as if that court case he had been handling had gone against him. One day they would learn to appreciate where the real astuteness in the department lay, and put Martella in charge of the more complex, tantalizing investigations. Then she would show them. One day.

Burnside come out of his office. 'Well? Chucked it out, did they?'

Dashwood kept his face straight for a long moment, then grinned. 'Nope. Fifteen years.'

Burnside and Carver cheered.

'Nice one, Michael. This calls for a little light refreshment. You're buying.'

'Mm. I thought I might be.'

Jimmy Carver did not need telling twice. He was on his feet, following the other two men through the door. 'You coming for a drink, Viv?'

'She's far too busy,' said Burnside over his shoulder.

'I'm far too busy,' said Martella grimly. 'Thanks.'

So Dashwood the smoothie had pulled it off. She could only hope that Tosh Lines would come a cropper, and that next time she would be the smooth, practised interrogator down in the interview room showing them all how it ought to be done.

The daydreams continued as she propped herself against a filing cabinet and began shuffling Burnside's papers into some sort of order.

DC Lines started the tape machine and settled himself in a chair opposite Terry Pearce. He belched once, deciding to stick to corned beef sandwiches in future and steer clear of cheese and onion. There was no need to apologize to his companion for the belch. Pearce, a scruffy and scurfy man in his mid-twenties, was indifferent to the niceties of existence. Right now he was doing his best to look indifferent to everything else as well. After a long contemplation of the opposite wall he answered Tosh Lines' stare with his own blank, unyielding gaze.

At last Tosh made a move. 'I want you to take your time, lad. Think carefully before you speak.'

Pearce's oddly remote, washed-out eyes gave no hint that he was likely either to speak or even to think.

'There's no rush,' said Lines. 'I've got all day.' When there was still no reply he added: 'Just as well, eh?'

The recorder went on wasting its reel of tape on a silence broken only by an occasional wheeze from Pearce, and the rumbling of Tosh's stomach. The whole thing was a waste of time. Pearce would crack sooner or later: he hadn't got the stamina to hold out against determined questioning. The robbery last night bore all the marks of his destructive clumsiness, and right now he was having difficulty in suppressing a yawn. His eyes watered with tiredness. He had done it all right, and Tosh knew it.

The only trouble was that at four o'clock the custody officer would insist on the regulation review, and if Pearce hadn't talked by then he might well succeed in talking himself out of Sun Hill.

Tosh said: 'All right, then. What were you doing last night, Terry?'

Pearce struggled with another telltale yawn.

'It's a very simple question, Terry. Shall I repeat it, or shall we take it as read?' After a pause he went on: 'I think I'll repeat it. Just in case you missed it. What were you doing last night?'

'Sheena.' It was little more than a contemptuous mumble.

'It speaks! It's a miracle.' Tosh joked harshly to conceal his relief that the dialogue had started. 'So you were doing Sheena, were you?'

'I was *with* her.'

'Sheena Rossi, is this?'

'Yeah.'

The detective constable suppressed a shudder. He had heard many a sentimental story about tarts with hearts of gold, but there were not many in real life, and Sheena Rossi was certainly not among them. Only a desperate man with reckless lack of concern for his health would seek Sheena's favours; if that was the right word for them. Thin to the point of emaciation and with a skin like soggy brown paper, the only thing she had to offer was willingness – at a price. Even thinking about her made Tosh Lines itch in places he preferred not to scratch.

He said: 'She'll tell the same story, will she?'

'Yeah.'

'You're wealthier than I thought. Or does she take credit cards now?'

Terry Pearce had apparently exhausted all his reserves of light conversation. He resumed his study of the far wall.

Tosh eased himself up from the chair, switched off the recorder, and ensured that the prisoner was returned to the custody area.

'Four o'clock for review,' Sergeant Cryer reminded him.

There were times when it was not just Bob Cryer's beak

8

of a nose that made one think of a parrot, but his way of squawking the same dreary stuff over and over again. 'It's a doddle,' growled Tosh. 'But I've got a busy afternoon ahead.'

There was an appreciative whistle from Sergeant Peters as Viv Martella came along the corridor, heading for the canteen. Her plum-coloured suit brought out the deep, dark olive shadows in her eyes, and her hair was sleek in a way it could never have been if squashed under a uniform cap.

'Well, well,' carolled Peters. 'There's us thinking you'd gone to CID, and you're really off on a multi-million-dollar modelling job.'

'Very funny, sarge.'

Lines followed her upstairs to the canteen, bought himself a cup of tea, and settled at a table beside her. She was more attractive company than Terry Pearce, that was for sure. Perhaps overdoing it a bit, though. Plain clothes meant plain clothes, not a jacket and skirt quite as smartly cut as that, and heels that high. She would make an even more remarkable contrast to Sheena Rossi, when the two of them got together.

He led up to it gently. 'Know where the others have gone?'

'The pub.'

He felt a flicker of interest. Get things moving, and he might be able to get across there himself.

'How's it all going?'

'Fine,' said Martella glumly.

'Bit strange at first, eh?'

'You can say that again.'

'When I signed up in uniform all those hundreds of years ago,' he sympathized, 'all I wanted was to be a detective, too. Racing about on all the exciting stuff. Soon found out there's more to it than that. Lot more paperwork for a start.'

She nodded fervent agreement.

'You missing the relief?'

'Tell you what I'm really missing.' She pushed her empty

9

teacup away. 'Getting out. I've been up there for a week and I've only been out for sandwiches. And chips.'

Lines avoided her accusing gaze, guiltily remembering the quantities of chips she had in fact brought in for him. Hastily he said: 'Tell you what. Want to do a job for me?'

'Not if it's typing or filing.'

'No. Could you bring someone in for me?'

'Who?'

'Sheena Rossi. Know her?'

'Thin girl.'

'Thin? I've seen more meat on a butcher's biro.'

'She's a tom down Wharf Road. That the one?'

'That's the one. She's on police bail. Hasn't reported in. I need her before four o'clock. Terry Pearce is up for review then, and she's his alibi.'

Martella began to cheer up at the thought of action. 'No bother,' she said. 'It's only round the corner.'

'Just as well, too. There isn't a spare car until tomorrow. Right. See you back here about three, then.'

When she had gone, Tosh strolled downstairs and out across the yard. Or, rather, he began strolling across the yard only to find himself involved in a maze of crates and scaffolding poles. The thought of the pub inspired him, like a rat in an experimental labyrinth, to seek a quick exit; but brought him up against the side of a portakabin which he was quite sure had not been there first thing this morning. It must all be part of the refurbishment and expansion of Sun Hill police station, threatened for many months but now being put into effect. Life at Sun Hill already had its fair share of chaos. It looked as if things were going to get a lot worse before they got better.

After two false trails Tosh fought his way free, and broke into a thirsty trot as he saw the pub door ahead.

Burnside wasted no words of welcome. 'What about Pearce?'

'Says he was with Sheena Rossi all night.'

10

'Hope he's got medical insurance. You on your way to pick her up?'

'Viv's doing it for me.'

The DI looked less than happy. 'You sure about that? Sheena's not a cuddly toy. She's a walking razor slash, that girl.'

'Viv'll manage.' Tosh tried to sound confident. 'Look, I'd have brought her in myself, only I've got all these chores.'

'What chores?'

'Thought you'd never ask, guv,' said Tosh. 'I'll have a pint.'

Viv Martella stood back from the mirror in the women's toilets. Whipping out her warrant card when required was not going to be such an easy, automatic gesture as it had been in the past. The pockets in her suit had not been designed for such things. She tried it from one pocket, but the angle was a bit awkward. Her handbag was worse: by the time she had opened it and dived a hand in, any potential villain would be legging it far away down the street.

June Ackland emerged unexpectedly from a cubicle. Martella swung towards the washbasin and began washing her hands.

'Enjoying life with the boys?' asked June with a brief side-long grin. 'Burnside keeping his hands off you?'

'Don't know whether to be relieved or insulted.'

June stood back and eyed her up and down. 'I love the outfit. But isn't it a bit too good for work? It'll get spoiled.'

WDC Martella was beginning to have her own secret doubts, but hastened to override them. 'I'll be careful, don't worry.'

She took a last surreptitious glance at herself in the mirror, and was rather pleased by what she saw.

It was no more than a ten-minute walk to Wharf Road, and there was no wasted time when she got there. Sheena Rossi was conveniently standing in a doorway. It was not all that much of a coincidence: the site was one she had used

11

hundreds of times before. Her stance, too, was the same as usual. She seemed to bend her narrow knees ever so slightly as if to ease the strain, so that her head tilted a few inches forward and her lank, straight hair spilled a few strands over her gaunt face.

Martella crossed the road, giving herself plenty of time to get her warrant card out and display it.

'Sheena Rossi?'

'Huh.'

'Could you come to Sun Hill station with me to answer some questions?'

The sour, drawn face twisted into a supplication which could have been tragic, if you hadn't been on the beat long enough to know how easily the agony could be turned on.

'I know I didn't report in.' The whine was humble and repentant. 'I had some problems.'

'We just want to talk to you.'

'What've I done? Come on' – the head leaned even further forward, a foul breath wafted across Martella's cheek – 'tell me.'

'Just come along, please. Don't make a fuss.'

'Don't pull me in. You can't.' Sheena Rossi produced a convincing whimper. 'Listen. Just listen to me. I'm not well. I've just come back from the doctor, right? Honest. You know what he told me? I'm dying. I've got cancer. Here, inside.' She laid her bony right hand across her flat chest. 'Do I look well? *Do* I? Please, don't take me in . . . please . . . I can't go. Just leave me here. I won't cause any trouble, straight up. He's given me six months to live. Six months. I just want to die in peace.'

It was poignant. Moving. Martella was unmoved.

She said: 'You finished yet?'

Rossi was quite genuinely shocked. 'I don't believe it. You . . . you hard bitch.'

Martella shrugged. She had been tempted to join in the last few lines, but had been afraid it might spoil Sheena Rossi's performance. Rossi had forgotten being pulled in before. A

12

WPC in uniform must have looked very different from this stylish WDC. The story then had been exactly the same. Only that was nine months ago, and Rossi's six months of life had apparently been extended by some medical or heavenly intervention.

'Come on, Sheena.'

Martella reached for Rossi's arm. Thin and limp the girl might look, but her reactions were by no means limp. She jerked her arm away, shot out from the doorway, and was off down the neighbouring alley like a wild cat with a mongrel after it. Which was probably how she regarded all policemen and policewomen.

It was now that Martella realized the disadvantages of her stylish attire. In uniform she had encountered few difficulties in belting after a suspect. Now her heels threatened to twist between the uneven slabs of the alley; her jacket was too tight; and two of the buttons of her skirt popped as she broke into a run. Sheena Rossi, in jeans, was way ahead. She scaled a wall and threw herself nimbly over into a back garden. Martella went at the wall at the same pace and heard a faint tearing sound down her left thigh. Beyond the garden were two low fences. Rossi cleared both of them like a champion hurdler. Martella found it necessary to climb gingerly over. By the time she had run through a shop and panted out into the street beyond, Rossi was already waving to a group of men leaning against a Cortina by the kerb.

'Quick. It's the filth.'

One man sprang into the car and threw open the passenger door. The others scattered. As the car roared away, Martella reached instinctively for the radio that had always been at her shoulder. Only it was not there any more. Such a thing would not have gone well with her present outfit.

Desperately she looked around. A few curious passers-by smirked sheepishly. They had seen what had gone on, but didn't want to know too much. Not round here, they didn't.

13

A minicab was just about to edge away from the kerb after delivering two passengers outside a furniture shop.

Martella flashed her warrant. 'Police. Follow that Cortina.'

The cab driver, a little man with a face grown cheerful from being rude to anyone who came within range, leered at her in utter disbelief. 'You've got to be kidding, darling.' He drove off with a happy wave.

She tried to flag down two passing cars. The drivers, both of them small middle-aged men, looked at her with an alarm which spoke of large wives waiting at home and storing up resentments which the slightest excuse would trigger off. Each accelerated and escaped at a speed which would have excited the attention of any traffic policeman who happened to be in the vicinity.

A third car swung in to the kerb. Its driver could not have been more than nineteen or twenty. He eyed her up and down, and was clearly not in any fear of a wife at home.

'Police,' she said crisply. 'Give me a lift, will you?'

'No problem.' He eyed her legs as she swung into the passenger seat. 'Going far?'

She bobbed to and fro, leaning against his shoulder as she tried to see between the traffic ahead. The driver did not object to this hazard. His wandering gaze alerted her to the fact that her skirt had split up to the thigh.

She said: 'That blue Cortina. Turning left. Get after it, will you?'

'Anything you say.' His eyes continued caressing her more obvious parts. 'You sure you're a policewoman?'

'Want to see my warrant card again?'

'No, I'll make do with what I've got. My name's Dean, by the way. Dean Platt. With a double T.'

She would have been a lot happier if he had kept his eyes on the road. Tugging at what was left of her skirt, she leaned forward, willing the car on to catch up with that blue one ahead. A Datsun cut in suddenly between them, and she cursed. Platt looked at her with growing appreciation.

14

'Try a right again here,' she snapped.

Obediently he swung right, then braked hard. They were in a dead end.

There was no way now of picking up the trail. Martella sighed. 'OK. That's that, then. Can you take me back to Sun Hill?'

'Sure. No problem.'

Platt leaned back, and now she had to look at him rather than at the road ahead and the swirl of traffic. He had moist lips and eyes which he undoubtedly thought were inviting. His hair had not been cut but, as they said, styled. It did its best to embellish his low forehead and the remarkable smallness of his ears. Martella found the prospect unappetizing, and looked away.

Slowly he reversed out. 'What does your husband think of you being in the police?'

'I'm not married.'

His lips rubbed hopefully against each other. 'Your boy friend, then?'

'Which one?' she said curtly.

'Work long hours, do you?'

'Sometimes.' She had had enough of this. She felt drained, not keen on getting back to Sun Hill with the news that, come four o'clock, Tosh Lines was likely to lose Terry Pearce, but even less keen on sitting beside this Dean Platt while his eyes crawled over her and down inside her blouse. 'Can we head for Sun Hill, please?'

'When d'you finish?'

'Depends.'

'When d'you finish tonight?'

'Late.'

'Doing anything after work?'

'Yes.'

'What about tomorrow night?'

Martella looked despairingly at her watch. 'Look, can you just get me to Sun Hill – *please*?'

'Tomorrow night?' he persisted.

15

'No, thank you.'

'Name an evening. Any evening.'

'Look, Mr Platt, I'm just doing a job, OK? I'm in a hurry, I've got a lot to do. Can you just drive me back to the station?'

'Can't I see you again?'

'I really don't think so.'

Platt was slowing, automatically watching the road ahead but more concerned with sorting something out right here in the car. 'So that's it, is it?'

'Afraid so.'

He braked, and bumped the car up a few inches over the kerb. 'I've just remembered something. I've got something urgent to do.'

'But you're not ... I mean, you can just drop me back at the −'

'I can drop you,' he said thinly, 'right here. Come on, you'll have to get out.'

'Oh, come on, now.'

'Out, I said.'

'This is stupid.'

'And guess who's the stupid one.'

He leaned across her to open the door, letting his elbow brush her breast. As she swung out on to the pavement he gave her long, sleek right leg a regretful look.

She said: 'Thanks for nothing.'

'You shouldn't promise what you can't deliver.'

'What are you talking about?'

He nodded towards her torn skirt.

Martella straightened up. He could not resist leaning over for another look as he reached for the door handle.

'You should grow up.' Her temper mounted. She was furious with herself, but even more furious with him for gloating over her when he should have been focusing on that blue Cortina. 'You'd better not put a foot wrong on this manor, Mr Pratt.'

'I told you, my name's Platt.'

16

'Not so far as I'm concerned. Let me tell you, you've got an enemy for life.'

'And you,' he yelled as the door slammed shut, 'have got a long walk.'

Martella looked wretchedly down at her wrecked skirt and battered shoes; and began that walk.

Two

Cathy Marshall shifted a stack of files from one side of the Local Intelligence Office to the other; and then, finding she had blocked her own way to the door, moved them back again. Preparations for a temporary transfer of certain documents on current cases to Barton Street station while Sun Hill was being rebuilt posed a growing number of problems. Barton Street custody area would have to accommodate not just Sun Hill duty officers but relevant charge sheets and files; but at the same time Sun Hill CID, due to be shifted into a portakabin, might want those same files close at hand. It was a matter of the collator's judgement which papers should go and which be kept here. Marshall was beginning to doubt that judgement. She felt that for the past three days she had been dislocating rather than collating.

Viv Martella appeared in the doorway, and edged her way round a teetering pile of boxes. She had looked cool and smart when Marshall passed her this morning. Now she was dishevelled, and there was a tear in her skirt.

'What can I do for you?' WPC Marshall was in no mood to be her usual friendly, helpful self.

'You got anything on Sheena Rossi?'

The collator snorted. The saga of Sheena Rossi came in a number of volumes: soon, she thought, to be a major motion picture.

'How much d'you want?'

'I've got to bring her in.'

'Take your running shoes.' But automatically she was moving to the relevant filing cabinet, riffling through the cards,

18

and producing the right one in a matter of seconds. 'What d'you need? Address?'

Martella shuffled awkwardly. 'It's a bit embarrassing. I lost her. Or she she lost me.'

'Oh, I see. You've already had a go, then? I suppose she gave you the usual hard luck story?'

'You know about that?'

Cathy Marshall refrained from boasting that she knew everything about every villain and layabout on this manor. Sheena Rossi was one of the more predictable characters. She wasn't called 'Nine Lives' for nothing. For as long as anyone had known her she had bewailed having only six months to live.

'So what happened?'

'She legged it. And we only wanted to question her. About Terry Pearce. She's not in any more trouble.'

'And you thought it'd be a doddle.'

'We need her by four. I promised Tosh Lines.'

Marshall was growing impatient. Today she had no appetite for hard luck stories, whether Sheena Rossi's or Viv Martella's. 'You shouldn't promise what you can't deliver.' What she did have an appetite for, right now, was a bit of lecturing. Naturally efficient and organized, she could never really understand why other people weren't. For all her recent promotion and would-be tough mannerisms, Viv was still a bit naive. The occasional jolt would do her good. 'You should've come to me first,' Marshall said. 'Local Intelligence. Here to help. Can't help if you don't ask.'

Martella looked as if she was going to snap back, but thought better of it. 'Well, I'm asking now, Cathy,' she said meekly. 'OK? Where would she go?'

Marshall felt herself in control of the situation. She savoured it for a moment, then relented. 'That depends. She needs money and she needs her medicine. Whatever happens she'll try to get back home. Where was she heading when she lost you?'

'She was driven off in a blue Cortina by a bloke she must have known.'

'Get the number?'

Martella studied her feet sheepishly. 'No.'

Marshall turned back to the filing drawer. Something ticked at the back of her mind. She drew out a card, and nodded. Danny Pearce had a blue Cortina. Danny: Terry Pearce's brother. Triumphantly she handed the card to Martella, who looked gloomy rather than gratified as she copied the address on to a slip of paper.

'It's miles away.'

'If he's not there you can try Maltese Mike's place in Kirby Street. Danny does the odd job for him. So does Sheena. Right. Want some uniformed assistance?'

This time Martella did spark back. 'No, thanks. I can manage.'

In those clothes? Cathy Marshall kept the comment to herself. 'Hope I've been some help.' She closed the filing cabinet and turned back to the folders she had dug out from the back of the shelf. Time for decisions. Then she realized that Martella had not left the room.

'Cathy, have you got your car here today?'

'Hold it –'

'All the others are out.'

'Mine's not insured for prisoners.'

'I really don't want to mess this up,' Martella implored. 'Please. It's important.'

Marshall brooded for a moment. Then she dug her bag out from beneath the accumulation of documents on her desk, and threw the car keys to Martella. She felt she deserved one last dig. 'If you'd just come to me in the first place –'

'Thanks, Cathy.' Martella made her escape.

Smoke from Dashwood's panatella wreathed above the line-up of empty glasses on the table. DI Burnside glanced at his watch, but was reluctant to order them all back to the station. They had something to celebrate today, so why not keep on celebrating? He leaned back in his chair and gazed expansively around the bar.

Four young men on the far side of the room caught his eye and quickly looked away. One glanced furtively back after a few seconds, then leaned forward to mutter to his mates.

Burnside's feeling of well-being began to evaporate. His instincts told him there was something dodgy about that little group. Drugs, maybe? It was all drugs nowadays. One stinking case after another. Once the main aggro on the manor had been petty gangs breaking one another up – which left less trouble for the Force to cope with – or muggings in back alleys. Still some of that around, but unfashionable. Now everything was tied up in one way or another with drugs. He hated it. You could tell the reek a mile away.

Dashwood had noticed his absorption. 'Want to try 'em, guv?'

'Maybe.'

Burnside finished his drink, but made no immediate move. Abruptly two of the young men got up and went into the toilets. That was the trigger. The DI was on his feet, heading for the toilet door.

'Come on, let's have a chat. Tosh, you can stay here and look after the drinks.'

'I've got to go. Viv'll be back with Sheena.'

'In a minute. Tell you what, you can buy us another round if you want to.'

Burnside, Carver and Dashwood swung back the two doors and went into the toilet. There was no sign of the two young men. Two of the cubicles were empty, but the one in the middle was occupied. Burnside thumped his fist on the door.

'Police. Come out.'

Carver and Dashwood went into the cubicles to either side, and stood on the seats to peer over.

The centre door opened and a worried, stooped old man came out. Burnside, startled, stepped back. Dashwood

21

jumped down and dashed towards the fire exit. It opened on to a narrow side street: an empty side street.

Burnside sniffed. He had been thinking about the smell of drugs, but this stench was something worse.

Jimmy Carver leaned over the large bin by the door. He wrinkled his nose, dipped into the bin, and brought out a Sainsbury's bag. When he opened it, the aroma wafted even more powerfully across the confined space.

In the bag were the hands missing from the Rosebery Park killing.

Viv Martella stopped at a shoe shop and bought herself a new pair of trainers. The effect, with her smart jacket and the slashed skirt, might be incongruous but at least she could move more briskly if Sheena Rossi tried any more wild sprints into the distance. Provided she could find Sheena again in the first place.

The locality was not one she had been familiar with. All the run-down streets looked the same. Some did not even have name plates to identify them. She slowed Cathy's Metro on a corner, ignoring an impatient hooting behind her, and tried to decide whether it was worth going down the long crescent, perhaps getting even more hopelessly lost.

Then she saw Danny Pearce's car. Pearce and Sheena Rossi were leaning on it, talking to another man. It looked as if they were haggling over some deal or other. Whatever it was, it was bound to be unsavoury. They were so engrossed that they did not see the Metro slide to a halt a few yards away. Martella was about to get out when, without warning, Pearce and the girl got into the Cortina and drove off.

The crescent ended at traffic lights on the main road. The lights were changing as Martella approached, but she accelerated wildly round the corner, terrified of losing the car ahead. At a pelican crossing she had to brake hard as an old lady hobbled across the road, managing to drop her bag and slowly pick it up on the way.

It soon became obvious where Pearce and Rossi were

22

heading. Martella relaxed. She was a few hundred yards behind when the Cortina pulled up outside Maltese Mike's strip joint. This at least was on territory which Martella had paced out in the past. Nothing much had changed, except perhaps that Mike's club looked even sleazier than before.

Martella drove past and parked round the corner. When she walked back to the front of the club, a black youth was leaning on Pearce's car, smoking a large joint. He eyed her up and down as she approached, shaping up a leer which disappeared as she flashed her warrant card. The joint dropped from his hand and fell into the drain at his feet.

'I ain't done nothing,' he protested, frantically waving the blue curls of smoke away.

Martella looked at the car. The driver's window was open. 'This your car?'

'Nothing to do with me. Never seen it in my life before.'

'Open the bonnet, will you?'

'I told you, it's not my car.'

'Just open it.'

The youth looked fearfully around, then opened the car door and reached in for the bonnet release.

Martella liked to consider herself a good driver, but had never claimed to understand a thing about what went on inside the engine. Over the years she had picked up only a few phrases and ideas.

Now she said: 'Which is the distributor?'

He pointed. She wrenched the distributor cap off and slammed down the bonnet. Speechless, he watched her march into the club.

The room inside was dingy and filled with smoke. A few despondent-looking men sat at stained, battered tables with half pints of beer in front of them. A large and wobbly woman danced on the creaking stage to the harshly amplified accompaniment of a Cliff Richards disc.

Martella went to the bar. 'I want to see Mike.'

The barman leaned over to get a better look at her legs. He seemed pleased with what he saw. 'You auditioning?'

'Maybe. Tell me where Mike is, and you can watch.'

He went through a bead curtain behind the bar, and returned to motion her in. She found herself in a cramped back room, just as smoky as the club area. Pearce and Rossi were in a huddle with two other men. She remembered Maltese Mike, but as he slouched towards her he did not recognize her in her present garb.

'You the new girl?'

'You *could* say that.'

The sound of her voice made Rossi look round. In an instant she and Pearce were on their feet, racing for another door. Beyond it was a succession of small rooms. In hot pursuit, Martella nearly trod on a couple snogging on the floor, and overturned a card table. There was a lot to Maltese Mike's place that could bear further investigation. But right now she had other things to attend to.

Pearce had shoved open a window in the corridor. He and Rossi scrambled through. Martella followed them out and round the corner, where the black youth was trying to fish his joint out of the drain with a stick. He straightened up as Pearce ducked into the car and tried to start it.

'It won't start, man,' observed the youth helpfully. Even more helpfully he added: 'I'd try the distributor.'

Sheena Rossi dodged round the car and made off at speed. Yet again she was showing what a cracking pace she could manage when she was desperate. Knowing every back alley and yard, she went over a garden wall and through the hole in a hedge, under billowing lines of washing, and through the middle of a family of garden gnomes. A dustbin was kicked across Martella's path, grazing her shin.

They were out into the main road again. Now, thanks to her trainers, Martella was gaining. But Rossi still had a hundred-yard lead – enough for her to leap on to a bus as it drew away from the stop. Martella let out a breath of despair. But the bus was stopping at a pedestrian crossing. She caught up with it, trying to ignore the grinning faces of passengers peering out at this unexpected slice of real-life drama. Somebody on the lower deck began applauding. The conductor, an elderly man who had clearly clung to rules and regulations for many a decade, was outraged.

'You should never do that. Shouldn't jump on or off a moving bus. I ought to turf you off at the next stop.'

Still panting, Martella produced her warrant card. 'Shut up.' She looked inside the bus, but there was no sign of Rossi. She began to climb the stairs, holding on grimly as the bus lurched round a roundabout. Just as she reached the top, Rossi vaulted over the rail and slid wildly down, jumping straight off the bus. By the time Martella got back down again, the bus was accelerating. She rang the bell furiously.

The conductor could not believe what was happening to him today. 'What d'you think you're doing?'

'Can't you stop it? I've got to get off.'

'You'll have to wait, like everyone else. I don't know what the world's coming to, really I don't.'

Martella caught a glimpse of Rossi vanishing into a crowd of shoppers across the street. Wearily she sat down. Then she looked at the road into which they were turning, and felt a twinge of optimism.

'This bus go anywhere near Wharf Road?'

'Right past it.' The conductor hated to pander to this eccentric platform-hopper, but his professional pride would not allow him to pretend ignorance. 'Two stops.'

Got her, said Martella contentedly to herself.

The conductor was discontented with her smug smile. 'If you're staying on,' he grunted, 'I want to see that pass again.'

At Wharf Road he watched disapprovingly as Martella sprang off the platform and made her way towards the doorway where she had first seen Rossi. The step was cluttered with a couple of girls and a nondescript man who showed no interest in them or in anything else. They looked only vaguely interested as Martella pushed past them and ran up the staircase immediately ahead. She had pounded her way into a few slum buildings in her time, but this one must be among the prize specimens.

A girl with very red lips and a very red blouse over sagging breasts lounged against the banister rail on the first landing. Martella tried to look matey – all girls together.

'Which is Sheena's room?'

'Who are you?'

'Her sister.' It hurt to say it.

The girl eyed her sceptically, but then jabbed a thumb upwards. 'Next floor. On the right.'

Martella, breathing hard, climbed another flight and tried the door of the room on the right. It was unlocked. She pushed her way in.

As rooms went, it had gone downhill long ago. Paper was peeling off the wall, reeking with damp. Instead of curtains there were only sheets of black plastic drooping around the window. A few supposedly sexy posters had been pinned to the wall, but the effect was dispiriting rather than exciting. A few crumpled packets from takeaway meals had been tossed into a fireplace which had not seen a real fire for years.

On top of a chest of drawers were some ampoules and a plastic sachet of powder. Martella picked up a cluster of the ampoules.

Voices murmured downstairs. There was a sudden wild clatter on the stairs. Sheena Rossi came crashing into the room. Martella kicked the door shut behind her.

'OK, Sheena. Got you this time.'

Rossi stared for a second, her rheumy eyes wet with hatred. Then she darted towards the mantelpiece and pulled a syringe from a box, waving it in front of her like a knife.

'Come and get it, slag.'

'Don't be a prat.'

'Come on.' Rossi was crouched like a cornered animal, the syringe like a venomous tongue ready to spit and strike.

'I'm not a social worker,' said Martella as steadily as she was able. 'I'm not going to run away. You want a scrap? You've got it.'

'Hard, are you?'

'Try me.'

Rossi lunged forward with the syringe; and missed. Martella opened her right hand to reveal the ampoules. 'Want your medicine?'

Rossi gulped. 'Give 'em here.'

'Legal, is it?'

'From the doctor.'

'What about this?' Martella made a quick grab for the sachet and dangled it between two fingers.

'Gimme that.'

'Doc know about this?'

Rossi's teeth began to chatter, in rage or despair. 'Give.'

Martella said: 'You're coming in.'

'No.'

'Listen, scrag-end.' Martella had had more than enough for one afternoon. Tactful community police procedures had run out. 'We're not interested in you,' she snarled. 'You're someone's alibi. Understand?'

'Whose?'

'I'm not that stupid. Just come along and answer a few questions. With the right answers. And if you don't come with me now, I'm going walkies with this lot' – she swung smoothly aside as Rossi made a vain snatch – '*and* we'll have you locked up.'

There was a long, shivering pause. Martella knew she had won. Rossi was trying to keep up the defiant face, but it was crumbling round its gaunt edges. 'What if I come?'

Martella smiled her matiest smile. 'Maybe we can do a deal. You talk to my colleague, and we'll forget about this.' She waved the drugs temptingly under Rossi's nose. 'Or you can suffer.' She dropped one of the ampoules and crushed it underfoot. 'Oops.'

'You're a hard bitch.'

'Thanks.'

They went downstairs and out into the street. Sheena Rossi's bony shoulders were hunched even more wretchedly than usual.

'We'll have to walk,' said Martella.

'Where's your car?'

'Outside Maltese Mike's.'

Rossi allowed herself one spontaneous little simper of pleasure. 'Won't be for long.'

Martella was tempted to belt her one round the ears, but knew the trouble this could cause later. Without another word she hustled Rossi along the road and down the slope to the back door of Sun Hill.

It was ten minutes to four. Tosh Lines wouldn't be best pleased at cutting things this fine. But at least she had shown up with the goods.

Cathy Marshall was crossing the custody area from the collator's office. 'Just in time,' she greeted Martella. 'Is the car OK?'

'Er . . .' Martella thought it inadvisable to mention the car's present location outside Maltese Mike's. 'I think so,' she said lamely.

'You *think* so?'

Martella rushed Sheena Rossi towards the stairs up to the CID office.

Tosh Lines had just come back into the office, looking worried. For once his worries did not concern the state of his family finances, or the drinks he had been conned into buying.

'Viv hasn't been in?'

Dashwood shook his head.

Through the glass partition they saw Burnside answering the phone, shaking his head and then smiling. He put the receiver down and joined them in the outer office.

'Tosh, got some good news for you.'

'I can do with it, guv.'

'Your pal, Pearce. You don't need Sheena Rossi any more. Forensic have wrapped it up. Pearce left his prints all over the flat.'

'Thank God for that. I'll tell them downstairs.'

Tosh had not reached the door when Martella came in. She

28

looked very much the worse for wear. The fashion model image had come apart. Her hair was down, the split in her skirt was lengthening by the minute, and her trainers did not seem quite the image for the well-dressed lady executive nowadays.

Yet she appeared triumphant.

Burnside said: 'Looks like somebody's been for a bit of rough over lunch. Or are we shaping up for teatime?'

Martella was still panting, but managed to combine it with a lofty air. 'I was bringing in Sheena Rossi, actually.' She beamed at Tosh Lines, awaiting his gratitude.

'Ah,' he said.

'I'm not too late, am I? She's downstairs now.'

'Yes, well . . . There's been a development. We . . . er . . . we don't actually need her any more.'

Martella stared, stupefied. 'You what?'

'But thanks,' said Tosh eagerly, 'for bringing her in.'

'After all that?'

'We could do her for possession while she's here, couldn't we,' suggested Dashwood soothingly. 'I mean, she's usually got something on her.' He offered Martella a placatory smile. 'Could be your first proper CID nick.'

Martella said, hard and clear: 'She was clean.'

'Never mind.' Burnside strolled closer. 'At least it gave you something to do. Got you a bit of exercise.'

His hand slid down her back and patted her hard on the bottom. Martella wheeled round, livid with rage. This was the last straw.

'If you ever do that again, I'll break your nose . . . *sir*.'

Dashwood looked up apprehensively. Tosh Lines pretended to be interested in the state of his fingernails. Burnside turned on her his coldest, meanest, snake-eyed stare. Then he smiled.

'Welcome to the team, Vivienne.'

Three

The approaches to Chief Superintendent Brownlow's office were growing daily more perilous with twisted cables, lengths of metal and wooden panels propped at all angles. The chief super's temper, too, was daily growing more ragged. But Burnside, having negotiated an assortment of lethal-looking tools and climbed the steps into the portakabin, found himself confronted this Tuesday morning with a smile and, for once, some good news.

Brownlow was at last prepared to give the go-ahead for Operation Middleman.

It had been hanging around for weeks while top brass argued, grumbled about lack of action, then forbade any action whatsoever. In the meantime the drug traffic in Sun Hill district increased. Kids on council estates were drawn into it; dealers made a mockery of the police's overstretched resources; and hospitals complained about the time spent on coping with junkies and with small-time crooks injured in vicious battles between the major operators. Now a pilot project had been sanctioned. And it had better work, suggested Brownlow's darkly frowning eyebrows. Time had been spent on drug raids in the past, and Sun Hill had come out with precious little to show for it. Sanctions for a wider operation would be forthcoming only if some convincing results could be produced swiftly in a tight little trial run.

DI Burnside began to bubble with anticipation. Every now and then he had shaped up ideas of his own, ready to move when given the chance. A new lead was needed, and he thought he could give it. They would target a slice of the business that had slipped through the net up to now. Just haul in a suitable suspect from a routine spin and then, this time, really hit the ground running and keep at it. All he had been waiting for was for Brownlow to commit men and time to the project. Now they had been given the nod, and were ready to go. He drove away from the congestion of Sun Hill yard in cheerful mood, ready to break the news to the team when they had mopped up their simple little assignment this morning.

All the omens were good. Detective Sergeant Alastair Greig and the two DCs had dragged Kenneth Stoller out of bed and delivered him safely to the Barton Street custody area, to be charged with burglary. It was a promising start to the day.

The only problem was that provided by the Barton Street team themselves. They resented having Sun Hill men dumped on them. Equally Sergeant Alec Peters, today's custody officer and usually the most amiable of men, was showing signs of strain in cramped conditions alongside dourly uncooperative colleagues who wanted only to see the back of him. They ought to be working together, following routines familiar to both of them. Instead, in a matter of a fortnight the atmosphere had become sour and aggressive, as if each station felt a possessive affection for its own villains and wanted no part in anybody else's. Already Sergeant Tom Penny had officially reported Sergeant Coles of Barton Street for maltreating a Sun Hill prisoner in one of the cells here, and earned himself and the relief an undying enmity. Whatever grumbles they had ever had about Sun Hill facilities, they all longed to be back there.

But Burnside refused to be depressed this morning. Greig commandeered an interview room and they had Kenneth Stoller wheeled in. Stoller was a lean man in his late twenties, with a ferrety face which had a certain seedy attractiveness to girls with whom he swaggered around in the evenings. In the cold light of morning there was more seediness than attractiveness. He was too dazed to argue. His fingerprints confirmed that he had committed the burglary of the corner shop, and the boxes in his bedroom had still carried the

31

shop's delivery address. It was too obvious: another Terry Pearce, another pathetic little rodent, hardly worth wasting the time for more than brisk, routine formalities.

This was not, however, what Burnside had in mind. As Stoller drearily admitted the crime, the DI was assessing possibilities. When he spoke, he saw that Greig was on the same wavelength, receiving him loud and clear.

'Well, you've been very helpful with the burglary, Kenny. Saved us all a lot of time. That's the way I like it.' Burnside turned casually to his sergeant. 'I'd be happy to charge him and see what we could do about bail . . .'

'Me, too.' Greig rose to the occasion. 'If it weren't for the drugs.'

Stoller, who had been sitting slumped and apparently uncaring in his chair, now shifted uncomfortably.

'Yes,' said Burnside regretfully. 'There's the drugs. Opens up a whole new line of enquiry. You could have been out of here and about your business by lunchtime, Kenny. But for the drugs. What can you tell us about that?'

Stoller wilted under his gaze, and turned without much hope towards Greig. Greig assumed his best Scottish puritan expression.

Burnside said: 'Remind me what you found in the flat, Alastair.'

'Crystals of cocaine.'

'Otherwise known as rock. Or crack.'

'Look,' whined Stoller, 'what was that about bailing me, then?'

'That was on the burglary charge,' said Greig icily. 'Where you've been helpful and saved us time. You're not being helpful about the drugs.'

'If you helped us out with the drugs,' Burnside contributed, 'then we could talk to the custody sergeant, find out how soon we could get through the formalities, and so on.'

Stoller was looking at neither of them. Into the unknown he said: 'Yeah, well, all right, the rock was mine. It was in my possession. That what you want?'

32

Greig shook his head. 'We already knew that. We found it in your flat. That doesn't get us very far.'

'A fair old quantity you had there, Kenny,' said Burnside disapprovingly. 'More than you need for your habit. Enough to make you a bit of a dealer.'

Stoller shot upright. 'I never said I was dealing. Never said that.'

Burnside silently consulted Greig, who kept up the act. 'I don't think we could bail him. He'd interfere with our enquiries if we let him out. He'd have to prove me wrong.'

'By *helping* us with our enquiries . . .?'

'Look,' said Stoller. 'What d'you want?'

Burnside beamed, and told him. And slowly, reluctantly, Stoller began to name a few names.

Half an hour later they were bowling in a CID car along a street with which Stoller was so well acquainted that he preferred not to be recognized in his present situation. Shrinking down in the seat, he made himself as inconspicuous as possible.

'You can drop me under that bridge.'

'I'll drop you when I feel like it, Kenny,' said Burnside. 'I've got words to say. You're on the streets now thanks to me. So from now on you're mine. Got it? If you're up to the waist in sewage and I tell you to stand on your head, you do it till I tell you to stop. Are you with me?'

Stoller nodded dismally. 'Now can I get out?'

Burnside had no intention of letting him go so easily. The names that had trickled out went some way to building up the background details; but he needed more than that. The target had to be the local small-scale crack factories, about which Stoller knew more than he was yet telling. It was something relatively new to Sun Hill. There would be a lot of bouquets thrown around if the whole thing could be nipped in the bud before becoming a permanent headache. Burnside wanted to be in line for the tributes, floral or otherwise.

He said: 'Those names you gave us back at the nick. Chances against any of them having gear on the premises

33

when we walk in through the door are a thousand to one. It's only a nit like you who'd stuff it under his pillow and go to sleep.'

'Well, all I can do is give you names.'

'No, no. More than that. More than just the names. I need a bit of a delivery.'

Anguish etched lines into Stoller's cheeks. 'You can't expect me to set people up for you.'

'You coughed your way out of the nick,' said Burnside inexorably, 'because you need to be smoking the stuff just as soon as you get your hands on it. And selling it. Tonight. Look at the state of you.'

'You don't know what you're asking.'

'Not asking. Telling. I want that delivery. I want you to ask for a delivery, and I want to know the time and the supplier, so that when we come through the door it'll still be cooking.'

The Sun Hill CID cabin was even more cramped than the Barton Street custody area, but at least the faces all belonged to the home team. Burnside was glad to see Roach and Dashwood. Things now were in his own hands, and he was confident of coping. The news that Chief Superintendent Brownlow wanted to see him as soon as he got back must mean something good, too: they wanted results, they would get them.

He made his way with increasing dexterity through the mess between one portakabin and another.

There was a stranger seated facing Brownlow. Both men got up as Burnside came in. The newcomer was a sandy-haired man with wide hazel eyes and a mildly ruminating smile. But there was something watchful and predatory behind that smile. Even before Brownlow spoke, the DI's intuition told him that the shine of the day was about to be dulled.

'Frank, I'd like you to meet Detective Inspector Wray . . . from the Drug Squad.'

It was like getting a kick in the guts. You assumed that the whole operation was a Sun Hill one, that any kudos would belong to your own team, and that the team could be relied on; and then you found somebody else was muscling in.

Burnside glared as he shook hands.

'Gordon Wray.' It came out very smooth and mellow. 'Good to meet you, Frank.'

'Gordon,' said Burnside guardedly.

'Right.' Brownlow was wearing his most devious, wary expression. Whatever games he played, he always liked to cover his back. 'Let's get down to business.' He waved them towards his conference table, far too large for its present accommodation. 'Gordon's our liaison with the Drug Squad on Operation Middleman, Frank. I want you to include him in all phases of the operation.'

Burnside fumed inside, but realized he would have to tread carefully. 'I did understand, sir, that we were going to play this whole thing very close to the chest.'

'My brief on this one is *liaison*, Frank.' Wray's smile was mollifying but unconvincing. 'It's your show. I'm just here to relate your results to the wider picture.'

'Now that you're quite clear on that, Frank' – *and you'd better be*, implied Brownlow – 'I'd like you to run our present ideas past Gordon.'

Burnside went over the scenario again, flatly and in a hurry. If this unwanted visitor found it hard to follow, that was just too bad. He admitted that up until now there had been a gap in their strategy regarding drug distribution. The crap, the users and shabby little street-level pushers, got swept up by the uniformed branch and the Crime Squad kids when they struck lucky. The top end of the market – the importers, the fat cats – were the province of Customs and the Drug Squad. But in the middle, the local wholesalers were slipping through the net. They moved fast from one squat to another before they could be targeted. The gear was only on the premises for a short time, so that if you did give them a spin you'd be lucky to find any.

Right now, in the case of 'crack', it was not just a question of distributors but of virtual small-scale factories, using

35

perfectly ordinary local kitchens to cook the cocaine hydro-chloride into rock. The set-up varied from place to place: in some areas the users were buying the coke and doing the cooking themselves. This was the sort of factory which was just getting established in Sun Hill, and it had to be trodden on here and now, before it became a whole part of the local culture.

'Crack is the buzz word at the moment,' said Brownlow, as if they were not already well aware of this. 'The press, the schools, the local council, they all want to know what we're doing about the so-called crack epidemic.' He stared earnestly at Burnside and then at Wray. 'Some good results would be very useful politically.'

Yes. *Politically.* Burnside caught the glimmer of a possible mutual rapport in Wray's eyes. Trust Brownlow to go for that angle: always twitching whenever a directive came down from the commissioner's office, dashing off for a round of golf with a local councillor or dignitary, ears cocked for the public relations aspect of a case rather than the hard facts his own officers were struggling to establish.

Wray said: 'So what's your method, Frank? It's got to be snouts in one form or another.'

'Sure.'

'With all the aggravation that entails.'

Burnside shook his head. 'You've got to know that scene. You don't use old lags who know the game and send you all round the houses. You pick the kids wet behind the ears, give those ears a bit of a twist so they're scared not to be friendly.' He shrugged. 'You've either got it or you haven't.'

'I look forward to seeing how it's done,' said Wray softly.

Burnside went on shaking his head. 'You won't *see* me working with informants, Gordon. But you'll see the results.'

He set off to assemble his task force.

By nine o'clock that evening they were all in place. Burnside and Carver had set up an observation post on the first floor of a derelict house facing the block of flats where Stoller had tremblingly promised there would be a drop. Alastair Greig had a notebook on his knee, ready to practise keeping a log with only one dim street lamp to help. All three were acutely conscious of DI Wray sitting behind them in the darkness, watching them rather than the street, and making God only knew what judgements on the operation so far. Somewhere out there in the shadows was a team under Sergeant Bob Cryer, and Inspector Monroe was in the alley alongside the target house with another group. After a good hour of this, they must all be getting very tired and pessimistic.

DCs Mike Dashwood and Tosh Lines were at least seated in reasonable comfort. Their car stood at the kerb a good way along the street from the flats. Some of the doors and windows at this end had been boarded up against squatters, but through one uncurtained window there was a glimpse of a naked electric bulb dangling from the ceiling. To fill in the time Dashwood was using his binoculars in the hope of finding something else – or someone else – naked. Tosh tried to distract him, not fancying the consequences of two police officers being reported as peeping Toms.

The PR resting on the dashboard cracked into life. 'Middleman Two from Burnside.'

Dashwood hurriedly passed the binoculars to Lines and reached for the radio. 'Receiving, guv.'

'Any activity in the street?'

'No movement, guvnor.'

They settled back into more waiting; and more doubts. But Burnside was not going to express those doubts aloud – not with Wray squatting there so attentively.

Carver wiped his eyes and crouched forward again, tilting the binoculars set on a tripod. A motorbike courier went past, but did not slow down. Somebody was standing in the doorway opposite, apparently just taking the night air, though this was not the healthiest part of the world for that.

'Could be Duggan,' murmured Burnside hopefully. 'Mark Duggan, that's who I was told. Looks as if he's waiting for someone.'

37

The man let himself back into the entrance hall, and the door closed behind him.

Wray said quietly: 'What time are we hoping for?'

'You can't ever be sure of a timetable with these sort of people. Late tonight, I was told: late on, for collection. Maybe after midnight. But if that's when my man collects, then the coke has to be delivered before then and cooked. And Duggan's been fingered as the cook. All right?'

'If you say so, Frank.'

Greig shifted awkwardly and edged towards the wall, as if to distance himself from any dispute which might flare up.

Burnside looked round at Wray. 'Wouldn't you be happier out there with Lines and Dashwood? I mean, when the balloon goes up they're the ones who'll be tailing the courier. That's your side of things, isn't it? Another rung up the ladder.'

'I'll stick with you, Frank,' said Wray equably.

Dashwood's voice broke into the room. 'Burnside from Middleman Two.'

'Receiving. Yes, Mike?'

'Be aware, a solo motorcycle has just turned into the street. Moving in direction of target.'

Burnside looked over Carver's shoulder into the street. Carver swivelled the binoculars on the tripod and picked up his objective. The bike was slowing, as the rider studied house numbers. It was taking him time: many of them had been obscured by grime or boarded over.

He went past the target. Burnside groaned. But maybe he was sweeping the plot. They were all tense and silent.

The rider turned and began to come back. He speeded up, slowed again, and then slewed in towards the target premises. When he dismounted he was carrying a standard courier's plastic satchel. He rang one of the bells beside the entrance; and waited.

This had to be it. Slags in squats did not get their eviction orders by special messenger at this time of night.

A light went on in the entrance hall. There was a delay

38

while somebody inside presumably inspected the caller through a peephole. Then the door opened a sliver, though still on a chain, and the package was delivered.

'Middleman Two from Burnside.'

'Receiving,' Dashwood answered.

'Pick up the courier and stay with him, Mike.'

'We can't keep up with a bike if he plays it dodgy.'

'Give it your best shot. I want to know where he goes, not nick him. But if you do lose him, blow it up to all cars on the main set.'

They watched the courier ride off towards the corner. As he turned it and disappeared, the dark shape of a car without lights slid in pursuit, the lights going on just before it was obscured by a row of buildings. Lines and Dashwood were on the move.

Wray got to his feet, looking expectantly at Burnside. He was taut and ready for action. Burnside deliberately kept him waiting, to show who was in charge here, then bent over the PR.

'Middleman units from Burnside. Go, go, go!'

They went. Ted Roach was beside Bob Cryer as their contingent rushed the target house with sledgehammers, axes and crowbars. From the side, Monroe silently indicated to PCs Quinnan and Stamp that now was the time to get over the wall, taking with them a light aluminium ladder. Once they were over, two more uniformed officers followed. The ladder swung into place against the sill of an unlit bathroom window. Stamp steadied it as Dave Quinnan went up.

Quinnan smashed the frosted glass with his baton, reached in and found the catch, and half fell, half climbed through. He jarred his hip against a washbasin, swore, and opened the bathroom door on to a passage adorned only with a length of frayed, faded carpet. Below him he could hear a heavy thud and then a storm of splintering noises as Roach and Cryer led the assault in through the main entrance.

A young woman was emerging from the kitchen with

39

a pan of boiling water. She turned her head towards the uproar from the foot of the stairs, then looked incredulously at Quinnan.

'Police,' he said, rather superfluously.

'Bastards!'

She swung the pan to throw the boiling water over his face and down the right shoulder. As he ducked, Melvin came rushing across the bathroom to crash into him. At the same time feet thundered up the stairs, the flat door split apart and collapsed inwards, and the place was suddenly jammed with uniformed men. Burnside and Wray elbowed a way through. Melvin and Quinnan had grabbed the woman and managed to hold her down long enough for WPC Datta to add a certain woman-to-woman ruthlessness which stopped the kicking and yelling.

Wray must have been growing impatient. Instead of playing the attentive observer, he abruptly pushed forward and on into the kitchen. Maybe he hoped to smell the stuff seething cheerfully away on the gas cooker.

The woman had been dragged off into a bedroom to get her out of the way. There was still a man in the kitchen: tall and gangling, but with a swarthy, battered killer's face and a killer's swiftness. It could be the Mark Duggan whose name had been passed to Burnside. Right now no one was worried about names. He was reaching for something from the wall by the cooker, and swinging savagely towards Wray with it. It was a large machete. Wray ducked, but was trapped against a cupboard door. Burnside launched himself across the kitchen and slammed a baton hard down on the man's arm. He howled with pain and dropped the machete. For good measure Burnside jabbed him in the ribs, so that he folded on to the floor.

Cryer was right behind with Garfield. 'Cuff him.' He waited until the handcuffs were on before glancing enquiringly at Burnside's baton.

'Always bring one for night duty,' smiled Burnside. 'And special occasions.'

Wray pushed himself away from the cupboard and took a deep breath. 'Cheers, Frank. I owe you one.'

'My pleasure, Gordon.' Burnside turned to the captive, held between Garfield and Young. 'Right then, Errol Flynn. Where's the gear?'

The snarled reply did not come under the category of willing co-operation with the forces of law and order.

Four

Mike Dashwood had been right. Following the motorbike was not an easy job for a car. The evening traffic was not all that heavy, but certainly enough to make it impossible to keep on the bike's tail. At the end of a quarter of an hour it had to be admitted that they had lost him. He could be miles away. The best they could claim was that they had his number, and Tosh was about to radio it in when they passed an all-night café and spotted a group of motorcycle couriers lounging outside. Dashwood slowed and craned his neck for a backward glance. He was sure that one of the bikes in the middle of the gang was the one they had lost. It seemed an unlikely setting, but drug runners maybe enjoyed a cup of tea like anyone else: they couldn't always be sampling the merchandise.

'I'm sure that's him. Let's pull him while we can.'

Tosh looked dubious. 'Burnside said not to nick him but just find out where he operates from. I mean, if we lose him again we can always trace him through the plates.'

'If they're kosher plates.'

'Right,' Tosh conceded. 'Let's do it.'

Dashwood did a U-turn which provoked protest from a number of horns, and slid on to the gritty area in front of the café. The bikers looked at him suspiciously; but the man on whom Dashwood had focused made no immediate move to run away. He answered their questions civilly, with a look of injured innocence which might have been carefully practised but had all the marks of sincerity. If he was involved in something shady, the shadiness seemed to be that of other people.

Dashwood and Lines went back dejectedly to Sun Hill, where Alastair Greig was writing up notes in a more legible handwriting than he had been able to achieve in the twilight of the observation post. Morosely they reported that the motorbike courier was just that: a legitimate motorbike courier. He had received a call to pick up a package from a man in a hotel in Finsbury Park. He was paid cash. The customer's description had nothing to distinguish it from a million other characters. Lines had checked with the hotel, to find that the man's name was Johnson.

'Very uncommon,' said Greig. When it came to dourness, he was the past master. 'So distinctive.'

'Paid cash in advance for a room for the night. They probably thought he was bringing a tom back.'

'And he hasn't returned yet?'

'Taken his case with him.'

'And you believe the courier thought it was an innocent transaction?'

'Why wouldn't he? After all,' Dashwood pointed out, 'we've no report from Burnside and the rest that it *wasn't*. Not so far, anyway.'

Burnside, Wray and Roach had gone through every cupboard, pulled out every drawer, and virtually taken the cooker to pieces. Uniformed officers prowled through the rest of the flat, finding no signs of anything other than the debris of what had clearly been a group of squatters. It was a miracle the gas and electricity was still on: hard to imagine who had paid the bill, or who in either local office had omitted to turn them off.

Inspector Monroe had ordered Dave Quinnan back to the station in the van to check on the scalding of his right cheek and a few inches of his wrist. Monroe had begun his working life as a miner, refused to believe that anybody without his background could ever have known what real hard physical work was like, and had a habit of putting the fear of God into superiors and subordinates alike. But genuine injury

43

and genuine trouble were things he knew about, too; and without ever letting his belligerent features alter by the merest fraction he would make sure his men got the right treatment, and as fast as possible. Having settled that, he wanted the current villains to get the right treatment as well – and fast, very fast.

The trouble was that no useful evidence had yet surfaced.

Monroe stood beside Burnside and studied without enthusiasm the fragments which had been dragged from the deeper recesses of wall-mounted units. 'Baking powder. They seem to go in a lot for baking powder.'

'Well, they would, wouldn't they?'

Wray was allowing the contempt of an expert to show through. 'This joint's well down market. They usually do the job in a microwave nowadays.'

'Hello!' Ted Roach had been standing on a chair, groping along the tops of the wall units. He reached out a wavering foot to get himself back to the floor, and held out a small package wrapped in brown paper. 'Must have slung it up there when we broke in.'

Burnside held his hand out, but it was Wray who moved forward to claim the package. 'Mind if I take a look?'

Burnside minded like hell, but kept a grip on himself.

Wray carefully peeled away the paper, to reveal a small plastic bag with white powder in it. He opened it and took a sniff.

Burnside could not resist the chance. 'Don't sniff too hard, Gordon. You're not here to enjoy yourself.'

'We'll want forensic on this.'

'Naturally.'

'But,' said Wray, 'it bears a remarkable resemblance to talcum powder.'

'That slag didn't try and cut your head off to protect a delivery of talcum powder.'

'Perhaps,' suggested Monroe in the background, 'he's sensitive about his personal freshness.'

The CID men glared at him.

44

Their glares were nothing in comparison with the chief superintendent's expression awaiting them first thing in the morning. It would have been possible to ascribe his wrath to the fact that all power supplies to the portakabin had mysteriously failed within five minutes of his arrival, and that the rain was slamming down noisily on the roof; but Brownlow had different intensities of anger, and this one was clearly personal.

'This is precisely what I'd hoped to avoid.'

'That flat had all the tell-tale signs of a crack factory,' Burnside protested.

A respectful few inches behind Burnside, Chief Inspector Conway curled his never particularly tolerant lips into a derisive grimace. 'Come to that, it seems to have had all the tell-tale signs of a cake factory. What it didn't have was any crack. Or any cocaine.'

His two senior officers were levelling their uncompromising gaze upon Burnside.

Wray said: 'Let's get this in perspective, sir. This was *not* a cock-up by Sun Hill CID.'

Burnside glanced at him in surprise. 'Dead right!'

'The operation was blown,' Wray continued steadily, 'and deliberately manipulated to discredit the Division's strategy.'

Brownlow scowled. 'So you're telling me we didn't balls it up on our own initiative, but were conned into it? I don't find that reassuring.'

'Me neither,' added Conway.

Burnside was in danger of boiling over. 'With all due respect, the game's not over till the whistle goes. The slags who've tried to have us over on this are going to regret it.'

'Frank, let me make myself quite clear.' Brownlow was looking straight ahead with disciplinary firmness, yet at the same time had the air of a man protecting his own back. 'We are not in the business of retaliation to save anyone's face.'

'We should bear in mind, sir' – Wray was playing the diplomat for all he was worth, though Burnside was as sceptical of his motives as of Brownlow's – 'that prisoners are still being interviewed. Charges may arise from last night's events.'

'That's as may be. But Operation Middleman is suspended until we have established what went wrong and why.'

Whatever else might have gone wrong, Ted Roach and Jimmy Carver had great hopes of Mark Duggan. In the Barton Street interview room he looked a lot less fearsome than he had done when wielding his machete. Now was the time to hit him, and hit him hard.

Carver began the proceedings. 'I hope you're quite clear about the seriousness of your situation. You assaulted a police officer with a deadly weapon.'

When Duggan did not reply, Roach weighed in. 'We could be looking at a charge of attempted murder here.'

'That wasn't an attempted murder.'

'You take a swing at a man with a machete – what would you call it?'

'Self defence.'

'This isn't a joking matter.'

'I'm not joking. Self defence, like I said.'

'How do you make that out?' asked Carver.

'You're in your home, right, and –'

'You weren't in your home,' said Roach. 'You were in premises you occupied without the permission of the owner.'

'Well, we ain't got no other home, so it's still home, innit? So you're at home, and the first thing you know there's breaking glass and then they're smashing all your doors down . . . you pick up the nearest thing and defend yourself.'

'The officers who first effected entry were uniformed officers.'

'I didn't see them. I was in the kitchen.'

'They identified themselves. They called out "Police".'

'Look, there's glass breaking and doors going in, loads of yelling and shouting, you can't tell who's saying what. Anyhow, the geezer who came into the kitchen, he was plain

46

clothes. What am I gonna do – ask him who he is, when he's just hammered my door down?'

Carver leaned forward. 'You said you picked up the nearest thing to hand.'

'That's right.'

'Why do you keep a machete close to hand, Mark?'

Mark Duggan shrugged.

'Expecting trouble?' Carver pressed him.

'Like you said, we're squatters. We been harassed before. Dogs, heavies, the lot – and I'm not talking about legal.'

'The truth is,' growled Roach, 'that you keep a weapon handy because you're in the drug business. Isn't that so?'

'I told you –'

'You're not afraid of being evicted, you're afraid of being ripped off or arrested. That's why the machete.'

'No.'

Carver glanced at his DS with feigned reluctance. 'It looks to me like an attempted murder charge.'

'Certainly does.'

The technique had worked with Burnside and Greig when they started this whole affair. No harm in trying it again.

'Attempted murder of a police officer,' Carver mused. 'We'd have to oppose bail on that one.'

'Very strongly.'

'Yeah, well,' said Duggan. 'You do what you want.'

'If you could persuade us it was something else ... if we could see our way to a lesser charge, things might be different.'

Duggan suddenly let fly a defiant yell. 'This is just a stupid *game*.'

'What's that mean, Mark?'

'I got nothing more to say. Nothing. Do what you want.'

The approach had failed to work twice. There was nothing to do but return him to Barton Street custody area for the time being.

Two desks had been squeezed into the space normally occupied by one. Sergeant Peters of Sun Hill sat at one,

Sergeant Coles of Barton Street at the other, like a couple of puppets about to break into a smartly manipulated comedy routine. There was little hint of comedy in their faces, however. Alec Peters carefully did not look at his companion. Coles, asserting his rights on his own patch, reached out imperiously for Mark Duggan's record. Carver handed it over.

Coles ran his snide gaze down the notes, then spared a glance for Duggan. 'Been a good boy, have you?' He had a face like a hatchet, and could have matched Duggan and his machete when it came to violence. The incident when he had lost his temper and beaten up one of the Sun Hill prisoners had not been forgotten; nor had the report which had been slammed in against him. Now, beckoning a uniformed constable forward to escort Duggan back to the cells, he pointedly ignored Peters but said in a voice which grated across the room: 'The sooner you get your nick in order and look after your own slags, the better.'

'That's what *we* think,' Roach assured him.

He and Carver went back to their Sherpa, squeezed into an unwelcoming corner of Barton Street yard.

'Not fond of us, is he?' said Carver.

'That's the way it goes.'

'You think it's safe leaving Duggan there with him, after what happened before?'

'Until we're back in Sun Hill for good, nothing's safe,' said Roach. 'And even there, the way we keep getting the rug pulled out from under . . . oh, I dunno.'

They got into the car and drove gloomily off, conscious of having nothing useful to report and no idea what came next.

DI Burnside was himself in no position to give instructions on what came next. He had already gone through that postmortem session with Brownlow, and was left to draw Roach and Carver into his own review of what had gone wrong. He stamped up and down the narrow confines of the makeshift

CID office impatiently as Ted Roach reported on the interview with Mark Duggan. None of it made any sense. Whatever yarn Duggan might be spinning now, he must have thought the gear was genuine and not just baking powder, or he would not have shaped up so aggressively when they burst in. If he and the girl had known the premises were clean, they could just have folded their arms and laughed at the police while calculating their compensation claim.

'If that gear was duff,' he fretted, 'you'd think he'd have sussed out the gear on delivery.'

'According to Mike and Tosh,' said Carver, 'the courier wasn't told to collect any payment from them. If you're not being asked for cash on the nail, you don't have to verify the goods on the spot.'

'So Mark Duggan and his tart were dropped in it same as we were.' Burnside brooded on this, and saw a spark of hope. 'That's a grievance we can work on. Where is he now?'

'Barton Street.'

Burnside grimaced. 'I wish I'd never heard of Barton Street.'

'That's what Mark seems to think, too,' said Carver.

'Eh?'

'Well, he was looking gutty enough after you sticked him, but when the uniforms told him he was going to be held at Barton Street he turned a whiter shade of pale.'

'That so?' Burnside was beginning to turn this over in his mind when he became aware that DI Wray had just climbed into the cabin. 'Mm. Let's have a private word, Gordon.'

They went down the stairs into the yard. A light sprinkling of dust fell from scaffolding high above, and they moved under an overhang of planking. Wray waited, oddly calm.

Burnside said: 'This'll be your hopping pot then, Gordon.'

'Sorry? I don't quite –'

'The place where you get off. I mean, Operation Middleman's suspended. There's nothing for you to liaise about now.'

'It doesn't quite work like that, Frank.' Wray was still calm:

49

like a sleepy cat, ready to purr or to lash out without warning when the moment arose. 'There's still a lot to be learned from what's going on down here. I'm tasked to stick with you.'

On top of everything else this was not the best news Burnside could have anticipated. Least of all did he like that remark about a lot still to be learned about what was going on down here. There was a nasty ring to it. He took it in, mulled it over, and forced a grin.

'Well, you're very welcome to a bit of our office space, mate, but you won't see much happening. I mean, I've got to be out on enquiries now. It's a bit sensitive, I can't take passengers.'

A hod carrier wandered between them. When he had gone, Wray too was trying to smile. 'I think we should have a quiet exchange of views, Frank. Outside the nick.'

'That might not be a bad idea.' Burnside gestured towards the gate. 'Because you're in severe danger of getting up my nostrils.'

He led the way out into the road, dodging round a cement mixer which showed every sign of being about to tip its load on his shoes. At the corner, walking just quickly enough to keep Wray a few steps behind him, he crossed into the park. A couple of young women pushing prams along the outer path came at him side by side, chatting so obliviously that he and Wray had to dodge on to the grass in order not to be run down. Far across the grass a dog was barking furiously, while a little man with a pink, imploring face called futile commands to it.

Wray came level with Burnside. He waited until they had passed a seat where a pensioner was shakily feeding crumbs to a cluster of pigeons, and then said quietly: 'There's a snout who put you on to the factory.'

'You don't say?'

'Don't prat me about, Frank. It was pretty clear the way you operate. And now your next move is to lean on the snout and see if he sold you a dummy.'

'If you know everything, Gordon, why bother to talk to me?'

'I want access to your snout.'

Burnside snorted contemptuously. 'Don't hold your breath till you get it, mate.'

'Look.' Now there was the hiss of something ready to pounce, lifting a claw in readiness. Here, maybe, came the real Gordon Wray. 'I came to see a drug bust. What I've seen is either an entry for the Nobel Balls-up Prize or something a bit naughty.'

'Meaning what?'

'Meaning,' said Wray brutally, 'that Operation Middleman could have been blown by a corrupt element within this Division. *This* one, Frank. Maybe your own snout knows about that, maybe not. You go off now on your own and put the arm on him, Frank, and it's going to look bad for you.'

Burnside stopped dead and grabbed Wray's elbow. His voice was low but murderous. 'You're a case, you are! You come barging into my firm, you hang around my operation like a spare wick at a wedding, and you end up making out I'm bent.'

Wray shook his arm free. 'I'm telling you about appearances.'

'And who the hell are you to stick your oar in? When it comes to appearances, let me tell you –'

'No. Let me tell *you*. Be advised, Frank. Put your cards on the table or it'll smell like you're stitching something up.'

'You don't give me orders, *inspector*.'

'Brownlow does, though.' As Burnside swung furiously away, Wray added: 'Or don't you agree with that? You think you're your own boss, or what?'

One thing Burnside quite definitely thought. He had had enough. He wanted this slimy intruder off his back and off the Sun Hill premises. Wray wanted to take it to Brownlow. All right, that was where they would take it. Burnside had got plenty of service in at this nick. He had produced results. Wray would find that he had plenty of clout.

They headed, not speaking, back to the yard and the chief superintendent's cabin.

Brownlow greeted them apprehensively, with a quick look at Wray as if asking a silent question. Burnside didn't like that look. It was just another of those expressions around here nowadays which were beginning to unsettle the whole routine.

He explained the position without wasting words. They were short words, too.

When he had finished, he expected Wray to put forward his own views, for what they were worth. But Wray stood quite still, waiting.

Brownlow said: 'Er . . . as you know, Frank, I'm only drawn into the details of CID's everyday operations with the greatest reluctance.'

'I've always appreciated that, sir.'

Brownlow fidgeted. If the phone had rung he would undoubtedly have grabbed it and kept a conversation going for as long as possible to postpone the awkward moment of declaring an unequivocal decision. But the phone refused to ring. He said:

'However, I do exercise an ultimate supervisory role over your activities.'

'Quite so, sir, That's why I've come to you.'

'Er, yes. In this case I have to make my decision in Inspector Wray's favour.'

'What . . .?'

'I am ordering you to give DI Wray full access to your informant. This matter has gone beyond the niceties of professional etiquette.'

Burnside struggled for breath and for words. He had heard some weird things from Brownlow in his time, but this was beyond belief.

'I'm sorry, sir, but I must ask you to reconsider.'

'That was an order, Frank.'

'Am I to understand that I'm no longer trusted in this station?'

'Drop it, Frank,' said Wray in an undertone. It made things no better.

'What you have to understand, Inspector Burnside' – the chief super was laying it on heavy now – 'is that Chief Inspector Conway and I are going to go through the records of Operation Middleman with a fine-toothed comb. What I desperately hope to find is that the operation was not compromised by an officer at this station. But until I do so, nobody is trusted. Now please co-operate with DI Wray as he has requested.'

'Yes, sir.'

It was the closest Burnside had every felt to utter, humiliating defeat. It had taken a long time for him to live down those old insinuations started by the Operation Countryman clean-up of corruption in the Force. Inspector Frazer had got round to spreading the truth of his commitment to the clean-up itself; but there were still some who only half believed her version. Now Operation Middleman had come along – another fancy name, and another muttering of suspicion which was bound to spread.

He left the cabin, knowing that Wray was on his heels and not trusting himself to turn and confront him.

Mike Dashwood peered down from the CID office window, watching the two figures disappear around a tangle of cables and junction boxes.

'What d'you suppose that was about? Looks as if he's been hit with a crowbar.'

'Wouldn't put it past Wray to be the one holding the crowbar,' observed Jimmy Carver.

'But I thought Brownlow had already given him his bollocking, and that was that?'

'Well, I don't know,' said Carver uneasily. 'But the way me and Ted have been reading the tea-leaves, if you've got shares in our guvnor, you want to unload 'em quick.'

Five

Unlike the trim grassy stretches of the park near Sun Hill, a large part of Canley Fields was scattered with unkempt patches of undergrowth and ragged trees and bushes. In the daytime it was not difficult to trace a path through the copses towards level stretches on the far fringe, accommodating a couple of swings and a slide. At night you could scratch yourself severely on thorns or twist an ankle in unseen holes and gullies. Anyone who slunk in there at night could be up to no good.

Which was why everyone in Sun Hill came fully awake on an otherwise drab, uneventful wintry evening, when Norika Datta at the switchboard got the sort of message they all dreaded.

'Sarge. Reported abduction. A young child.'

The area car raced towards the long road beside Canley Fields. A message had been received from a phone box: but there were three phone boxes in the vicinity. As Stamp switched the siren on and put his foot down, Melvin appealed: 'Sierra Oscar from Sierra One. Can you say which phone box, please?'

Sergeant Peters was quick to respond. 'Belfitt Road. Just along from the public toilets. One of the witnesses – name of Deacon – says you'll know him by his jeans and black top. The other's wearing dark trousers and a red ski jacket.'

The siren was cut off as they reached the end of the road and slowed down. It was a poorly lit road, and all the more sombre on the offside where tangled branches formed a barrier between the pavement and the fields. Grass had strayed out to crack a way through the paving stones. The block of public toilets looked gloomy and ill cared for. Beyond, the phone box slid into the beam of the car's headlights.

There was nobody near it.

'Come on, lads,' mumbled Stamp crossly. 'Where are you?'

He cruised on. A hundred yards ahead, an elderly Metro was parked under overhanging branches. As Stamp swung out to pass it, two young men crossed the road, one of them holding up his right hand. Their appearance matched Peters' description. Stamp parked, and he and Melvin got briskly out of the car.

'Mr Deacon?'

'Yeah, sorry. We went to see if we could spot anything.'

He was tall and held himself stiffly upright, as if to assert pride in some military training or other activity. He looked respectfully at the appearance of the two uniformed constables, which was a pleasant change from the sort of reaction that was all too common nowadays. The other youth was obviously the subordinate, the sort who could be lured into mischief and punch-ups if led on by his mate. Only they did not appear that type: Deacon exuded an air of almost over-zealousness to proclaim his virtues as a good citizen.

'Right,' Stamp prompted them, guessing which one would take it on himself to answer. 'What are we looking for? What happened?'

Deacon fulfilled his predictions. 'We were driving along, and there was this guy in the road in front of us, holding a kid.' He spoke as briskly as if he had been rehearsing every word while waiting for the police car to arrive. 'He ran across the road and into the bushes there.' Deacon pointed to a dark gap between dark foliage.

Melvin was reporting to Sun Hill and reaching under the dashboard for the seek-and-search light.

'Boy or girl?' asked Stamp.

'A boy.'

'And the boy was holding his hand, or what?'

The other young man spoke, fumbling slightly and glancing for approval at his friend. 'He had him by the arm. Dragging him. The kid was screaming.'

'And your name, pal?'

'Tuart. Rick Tuart.'

'How old – the kid?'

'Looked about seven or eight,' said Deacon. 'Blond hair.'

Melvin was carrying the lamp. They went towards the bushes. Stamp took the lamp and directed its beam through the dark mesh of branches where Deacon had indicated an opening. The light showed up an unmistakable trail of recently broken undergrowth leading into the copse beyond. Stamp trod carefully through. Then, over his shoulder, he waved Melvin back to the car to report.

'Sierra Oscar from Sierra One . . .'

'Receiving,' said Sergeant Peters apprehensively, waiting for the worst.

'Looks like a goer. There's a definite trail heading into Canley Fields.'

'Right. Could you ask the two witnesses to stay put. CID will come and fetch them.'

Chief Inspector Conway had been seen going out earlier that evening sporting a smart suit and his best charcoal grey overcoat. Officially the occasion was a working supper at which the main contractor for the Sun Hill refurbishment would host a discussion on arrangements for the next stage. In the eyes of the relief sergeant, Bob Cryer, it was no more than an expensive freebie; but it was not for him to do more than nod sceptically and take the number of the Wellesley Hotel in case of any sudden emergency.

Now there was an emergency all right. Inspector Monroe was alerted and took pleasure in summoning Conway respectfully back from the banquet, with a wry 'Drive carefully, sir.' Ted Roach and Tosh Lines tore themselves away from cups of tea and, in Tosh's case, a mound of cream cake in the recreation room, to set off in the direction of Canley Fields.

They brought back the witnesses Deacon and Tuart, who were now beginning to look nervous. It was clear they had never been in a police station before. A point in their favour, so far as the Sun Hill team were concerned; but it was equally clear that they would have to be handled carefully and discreetly.

Tosh Lines escorted young Tuart into the CID portakabin, apologizing for the cramped conditions. Tuart fidgeted, perhaps wondering how much more cramped his conditions might eventually become. Ted Roach picked his way over a junction box and some indefinable panels wrapped in plastic on his way to the beleaguered Sun Hill interview room. He waved Deacon amiably to a seat.

'Can we start with your full name and address, please, Mr Deacon.'

Deacon looked round the bleak room. 'Why have you split us up?'

Roach shrugged. 'Normal procedure. Avoids any confusion.'

He looked at Deacon, inviting him to answer the question.

It came with surprising, almost declamatory precision. 'Robert Alan Deacon, 24 Turnford Road.' And after that, he was as clear and authoritative as any police interviewer could have wished a witness to be.

Roach was uneasy without knowing why.

At the same time Tosh Lines was extracting a confirmatory story from Tuart. Unhappy with the atmosphere as he might be, and maybe wishing they had never made the phone call in the first place, Rick Tuart struggled to keep things straight. He told of the two figures they had seen in their headlights, of the man turning towards them for a split second and then speeding up and disappearing into the bushes. He gulped. 'Practically lifted the kid off his feet as he went.'

'Head lamps full beam, were they?'

'Had to be. The street lighting along there's useless.'

'And how fast were you travelling in the car?'

'Well, Robbie was driving, of course. But I'd say thirty, thirty-five. And Robbie braked when he saw them in the road.'

'How far ahead of you were they when you first saw them?'

Tuart wriggled on his chair. He was not keen to be too specific in case he got pulled up in some way he could not anticipate. 'Fifty yards?' he said tentatively.

'Then you stopped.'

'Yeah.'

'Why?'

Tuart looked surprised. 'Well, because it looked suspicious. And we heard the kid screaming.'

'As they were crossing or after they'd disappeared?'

'As they were crossing.' Tuart was beginning to sound resentful.

Outside, away from the questioning, other questions were being asked. Had any child been reported missing? So far there had been nothing in the immediate neighbourhood. Now the nit-picking routine had to begin. A full check of missing persons was needed, to try and establish age and description. Two panda cars were sent to the environs of Canley Fields. A helicopter might have been helpful, but it was after dark and in any case there was no machine immediately available. The public toilets were investigated, offering no joy. Conway, interrupted in the middle of a delicious lobster thermidor, shrugged off his overcoat and forced himself to turn his mind to a less tempting menu.

There was a lot of ground to cover. Canley Fields comprised roughly thirty acres of open space, much of it what could at best be called in a natural state – meaning that it was overgrown, and a receptacle for many of the tin cans, bottles, pram wheels and old newspapers in the district. There was no real perimeter fence. Panda 86 had already been stationed on the northern edge of the area. The group being assembled at Sun Hill would rendezvous with Panda 85 by the toilets. From there, ordered Conway, straining to make the big wall map come to life in three dimensions so that he could not only see but feel what the conditions were like, the team would fan out in a broad arc, moving towards the Prynn Road boundary. Three dog handlers and a Technical Support Group unit were on their way.

'Do *not* get in front of the dogs,' Conway emphasized. 'Otherwise, take your orders on the ground from Inspector Monroe or, as he directs, from Sergeant Cryer and Sergeant Peters.' Noting Peters' automatic twitch at the idea of being slung out onto the streets from the comparative comfort of the station, he said, with a longing aftertaste of lobster: 'I'm sure I shall be able to cope without you, Alec.'

'Sir.'

Ted Roach slipped into the room. Conway looked hopefully at him. 'Anything useful from the witnesses?'

'They're both being very cooperative, sir.' There was a sarcastic edge to Roach's voice. 'And there are no discrepancies between their stories.'

'You think it's a hoax?'

'I . . . well . . .'

'*Well*?'

Roach looked unsure and unhappy. 'I'm not saying that.'

Conway took a deep breath. Very firmly he said: 'Until proved otherwise, this is a genuine incident. A child's life could be at stake.'

The vehicles moved in, parking at angles so that they could direct their headlights deep into the undergrowth. There were Cryer's patrol car, Garfield's panda, and two dog handlers' vans. A TSG carrier joined them as the dogs were let out and directed to the edge of the fields.

The first dog and its handler began ploughing their way through the little local jungle, following the trail pointed out by Stamp. Unable to hold back from what might show up, Stamp himself followed with his seek-and-search lamp. Their information seemed to have been sound: the path was

59

clearly trodden for several yards ahead, then swung to the right, and went on again.

They all stopped in a trampled space. Could there have been a struggle here? The dog showed no great excitement, but paced on, still veering slowly to the right.

They emerged on the road less than fifty yards from their initial point of entry.

Stamp groaned.

Sergeant Cryer, who had just directed the two other dog handlers into the bushes, came along the road and confronted him.

'What's this? You going round in circles?'

'This is where the trail comes out, sarge.'

Cryer turned his attention balefully to the dog. 'Does he know what he's doing?'

'He's followed the scent of broken vegetation,' said the handler, aggrieved. 'That's all you asked him to do.'

'Point being, sarge,' Stamp intervened, 'when me and Ken first met the two lads they were midway between here and that bit down there.'

'Where you went in, you mean?'

'That's right.'

Cryer looked thoughtfully at the flattened twigs and grass where the trail reached the road. 'So they could have done this themselves?'

'Doesn't make much sense, but it's got to be a possibility.'

'I'll tell Monroe.' Cryer looked back at the doghandler. 'Can you fall in with the main sweep and see if there's anything else to be picked up?'

There was a growing sense of disillusion. Somebody, somewhere, had been wasting their time. But Conway had said it was to be treated as serious until they could be sure it had stopped being serious. And Monroe was on the spot to make sure they did just that.

Slowly a thin line of police officers marched slowly and methodically through Canley Fields. Sergeant Peters cut a swathe of brightness through the gloom with his torch, panning it from side to side in search of what none of them could define.

'I shouldn't be here,' whined PC Reg Hollis. 'I'm not equipped.' He edged closer to Sergeant Peters.

'Oh, do spread yourself out, Reg. We're supposed to maintain contact, not hold hands.'

'How can I see with only a dud torch?'

'Stick it in your mouth,' suggested Garfield in the background. 'Perhaps it'll run on gas.'

'I should be back at the nerve centre.'

'You should?' Peters was running out of patience. '*I'm* CAD sergeant. Total waste of time, anyway. I object to being kicked out in the cold for the sake of a wind-up. When I get my hands on –'

'Quick!' Stamp was calling. 'Over here!'

They heard him crashing through the undergrowth. The beam of his torch waved wildly in the air like a random searchlight. Peters swung off to the side, stumbled on a brief slope, and reached out to grab some kind of support, only to suffer a couple of sharp branches digging into his hand.

'Stop!' bellowed Stamp. 'Police!'

Feet stamped and cracked over twigs and fallen branches as the rest of the team converged on him. There was a sudden squeal like that of a frightened animal caught in a trap. Stamp's light disappeared as he lunged downwards in a heavy tackle. Peters reached the scene to find a seedy middle-aged man, his face pallid in the torchlight, wriggling helplessly under Stamp's weight. He wore a stone-coloured jerkin, navy blue trousers and a murky sweatshirt; and he looked very frightened.

They hauled him back to the road, doubled up and panting a maudlin protest. As they straightened him up in the glare of the car headlamps, Bob Cryer came hurrying along the road alive with expectation. When he saw their captive with Stamp's grip on his arm, he let out a groan of sheer frustration.

61

'But it's Gerry Coomer.'

'Yes, sarge.' Stamp sounded no better pleased.

'Not exactly his league, is it? Have you asked him what he's doing here?'

'Just getting round to it. And I'll bet it'll just be the usual.'

'Which isn't anything like what we've been looking for.'

'Still,' said Stamp hopefully, 'he's better than nothing, sarge.'

Cryer looked doubtful about this, but after a moment shrugged and waved dismissively towards the area car. 'Okay, take him in.'

Whatever those two young men had seen, or thought they had seen, or for some weird reason had misreported having seen, Gerry Coomer made no sense in it. But where was the sense, so far, in any of it?

Six

Outside the interview room, assessing the latest news – such as it was – Tosh Lines said sceptically: 'Tramping about in the bushes to lay false trails . . . a bit elaborate, isn't it?'

Ted Roach was wavering between belief and disbelief. 'All the best hoaxes are.'

'I don't think they're the type, Ted.'

'What do you want – goofy teeth and half-mast trousers?'

Lines looked glumly at the closed door. If there were any secrets behind it, they had been well concealed. The home addresses of Deacon and Tuart checked out; their motor was all right; neither had any form. 'This trail,' he ventured: 'it could be a complete coincidence anyway, nothing to do with the incident at all.'

Roach made a decision. At least they could put it to the young men baldly and see what sort of reaction they got. He would spring it on Deacon; Tosh Lines could have another go at Tuart. He went into the interview room and shut the door. Deacon, sipping tea at the desk, looked up with mounting displeasure.

Roach slumped into a chair. 'Funny thing's just cropped up, Robbie. The place you showed PC Stamp – where the man and the boy went into the undergrowth – there's a trail there all right, we've followed it through. But it doubles back on itself and comes out on the road again about fifty yards along. How would you explain that?'

Deacon shrugged. 'Dunno.'

'Only, when PC Stamp and PC Melvin first met you and Rick, you were midway between those two points.'

It did not seem to register. 'So?'

'You didn't see the man or the boy come out again at the second point?'

'We'd have told you if we had, wouldn't we?'

'And you and Rick didn't go into the undergrowth at all at any point?'

'No.'

'You're quite sure?'

Deacon was simmering up to a state of exasperation. 'Look, I've said before, we just went along the road a bit and . . . strewth . . .'

'What's the matter?'

'You're the matter, that's what. We try to help and you don't believe a word. You keep us here, you . . . . . Strewth, I wish we hadn't bothered.'

'But you did.' Roach tried to cool it. 'You've been very public-spirited and we're very grateful. So if I could just take up a little more of your time . . .'

Deacon sat back with a sigh.

Roach persevered, but he knew he was getting nowhere. They were trudging over the same old ground, over and over again. You had to do it this way, because there was always the chance of one little neglected fact, one little remark, emerging and throwing a new light on the whole business. Only in this case Deacon did not give the impression of concealing anything or of having forgotten anything vital. The only impression he gave was of being cheesed off. It was a feeling Roach shared.

The whole Sun Hill team was in the grip of frustration. WPC June Ackland had checked at the children's home, to find nobody missing. From the CAD room Conway chivvied Monroe, on the ground, at regular intervals as if sheer pestering would somehow provoke results. At one stage there was promise of a helicopter to sweep the fields with a powerful searchlight. Then it was announced that it was grounded with an engine fault.

Monroe sounded none too disappointed. 'What seems a good idea at the time,' he commented over the radio, 'doesn't always look so clever in the cold financial light of day, sir.'

Conway could do without this veiled criticism. 'I deploy the resources and I'll carry the can. It's not your worry, Andrew.'

'No, sir.' Monroe kept it respectful, though there was a waspishness behind his apparently innocent tone as he said: 'But not wishing to give lessons in sucking eggs, sir, have you considered the slight logistic problem we're going to have in just over half an hour?'

Conway glanced at the wall clock. It was eleven minutes past nine. 'I don't follow you, Andrew.'

'Just that the night relief will be arriving for duty, and we've got all their vehicles.'

'Um. Yes, thank you, Andrew.'

'And I've been thinking of some other consequences for efficient policing tomorrow morning, sir.'

'What consequences?'

'Well, tonight being a quick changeover, it's the late turn who relieve the night men in the morning. So if you keep the late men on till, say, two a.m., and they insist on their eight hours away from the station – to which they're fully entitled – there won't be a soul on the streets tomorrow till ten a.m.'

'Thank you, Andrew,' said Conway again, steadily.

He carefully did not look at Datta, at the console, but turned his attention to the wall map. A house-to-house check was being made to see if any boy had run off, or not returned. The children's home was being questioned in further detail by Ackland, and now there was a series of calls aimed at local hospitals. All of them slender chances; but there had to be a breakthrough somewhere.

Gerry Coomer showed no immediate sign of representing any breakthrough. Installed in the interview room, in the chair so recently occupied by Robert Deacon, he shakily clutched a polystyrene cup of tea but managed a show of indifference as Roach and Lines tried to over-awe him.

Roach began the attack. 'So what were you doing in Canley Fields, Gerry?'

Coomer sniggered. They knew perfectly well what he had been doing. They were mildly surprised that he did not simply make a reference to consenting male adults, accuse them of harassment, and demand to be allowed to walk out of here without further delay. Maybe he was saving that up for later. For a brief spell his curiosity was stronger than his nervousness.

'Why the heavy mob?'

'A child has been abducted, Gerry.' Roach took his time, loading every word with a heavy insinuation. 'A man was seen dragging a kid onto Canley Fields at around seven-thirty this evening. The man's description roughly fits you.'

Now Coomer was genuinely shocked and frightened. 'I want a solicitor.'

'The duty brief's not very good-looking,' said Lines. 'Not your type at all.'

'I don't care, I want him. Or someone. I'm not a child molester.'

'But you were there,' Roach persisted, 'at seven-thirty?'

'I am *not* a child molester, and you know it.'

'So what were you doing there?'

'You know that as well.'

'Who were you doing it with?'

'I want a solicitor.'

'Oh, come on Gerry, this is important.'

Coomer gulped. He took a last swig of tea, and wiped his lips miserably. Then said: 'Ian. I don't know his surname.'

'Let me have a guess,' said Tosh Lines. 'Mulgrave?'

'Oh, all right. Yes.'

'So where's Ian now?'

'I've no idea,' said Coomer sullenly. 'Home, I suppose. We were in a snug little hollow when you lot started arriving.

He got frightened and ran off. Thought you were yobs. They come looking for us sometimes, you know.'

'But you stayed put.'

'Until one of you lot trod on me, yes.'

'You didn't see or hear anything before the police arrived?'

Coomer thought for a moment, then waved a limp wrist. 'The occasional car. A police siren in the distance. You're always hearing those.'

'But nobody else going through the undergrowth? No voices?'

'No screams?' Roach added.

'Our little hollow's well tucked away.' Coomer summoned up a smirk. 'Sorry.'

Roach left the room for a minute, to find Chief Inspector Conway leaving the CAD room and heading in his direction.

'Any joy?'

'Definitely a non-runner in my opinion, sir.'

Conway looked alarmed. 'You haven't let him go?'

'No, but he wants a brief.'

'Get him one. Keep him happy, he may remember something. You may even be wrong. And what about the two lads?'

'We're giving them supper.'

'Do they want supper,' asked Conway meaningly, 'or would they rather be on their way?'

Roach got the insinuation loud and clear. 'Oh, no, they're quite happy to stick around.' He tried to keep it airy and inconsequential. 'Honest, sir.'

'Don't push it, Ted. If all we get at the end of this is a complaint, I shall be most annoyed.'

Norika Datta put her head round the CAD door.

'They've just finished Belfitt Road, sir. Continuing along the edge of the estate.'

'And nobody reported missing so far?'

'Nobody, sir.'

*

Extra TSG men had been brought in to comb Canley Fields even more thoroughly. The painstaking door-to-door enquiries spread down side streets and crescents and into closes where every door was opened suspiciously and queries were answered with fear or indignation. Whatever happened, there would be a lot of talk and speculation around the area by tomorrow morning; and the way things were going, little of it would be complimentary to the police.

An incalculable number of men would be needed to seal off Canley Fields completely. And if it was not thoroughly sealed, what was the point? Men were needed all round the perimeter for when their quarry was flushed out; and enough men were needed to flush him out in the first place.

Most likely, they began to feel, the abductor and the kid had already been through and gone. Or the man was cunning enough to lie up all night, not moving. Even the dogs would not find him if they did not know exactly who or what they were looking for.

But where did that leave the kid?

If there had ever been any such incident. If the man had ever existed at all . . .

Tosh Lines paid a quick visit to Ian Mulgrave, who corroborated Gerry Coomer's story in every detail. There was little reason to doubt him. 'They're both bent as pins,' Lines reported to Conway, 'but I've always found them very straight. If you see what I mean.'

Conway grimly had to admit that he could conceive what Lines meant.

He put through another call to Inspector Monroe. 'We'll give it ten more minutes, Andrew. Then I want a considered assessment of the situation on the ground.'

Defeat hung in the air. Also hanging in the air was the cloudy suspicion, growing more substantial as the night dragged on, that the whole thing was a put-up job. What was not clear was any reason for such time-wasting silliness.

As Tosh Lines headed thirstily for the canteen, Ted Roach said: 'Hold it. Roust our heroes out of there, will you?'

'We're not starting all over again?'

'Just fetch 'em, that's all.' Roach made his way to the CAD room and leaned over Datta at her keyboard. 'Norika, can you tell me the exact time the 999 call came through and started all this?'

She referred to her log. 'Nineteen-thirty precisely.'

'Uhuh. And how about –'

'But it wasn't a 999,' she interrupted. 'It was a direct call.'

'What – on Sun Hill's number?'

'Yes.'

Roach played around with this revelation for a moment, but could make nothing of it. Yet there had to be some significance somewhere.

Deacon had made the call. That much they knew, since he had quite clearly identified himself. Deacon had been the one in charge all along, with his mate doggedly trailing at his heels. So if there was anything to be learned, it was time to creep up on Deacon from behind.

Thoughtfully he went in the direction of the door to the yard and the CID cabin as Lines escorted the two young men, now looking thoroughly disgruntled, back from the canteen.

'Swap partners, shall we?' said Roach in an undertone.

'What for?'

'I'm not sure Mr Deacon likes me.'

'But what more is there to say, anyway?'

'You'll think of something,' Roach assured him, indicating that Deacon should accompany Lines to the interview room while Tuart went up the steps to the cabin. Inside, he said amiably: 'So, Rick, how d'you like police grub?'

Tuart did not seem to care one way or the other. 'Not bad.'

'Good. Now, at the risk of boring you, can we just go back to seven-thirty this evening? You saw the man and the boy. You stopped your car. You ran to the phone box. Then what?'

'We phoned.'

'You were both in the phone box?'

'Yeah.'

'But it was Robbie who actually made the call?'

Tuart nodded, as if this might surely have been taken for granted.

'He dialled 999?' said Roach.

'Oh, no,' said Tuart simply. 'He rang your number here.'

Roach tried not to look too concerned or too incredulous. 'You mean he looked up Sun Hill police station in the directory? A bit time-consuming, wasn't it, in an emergency?'

'No, he knew Sun Hill's number all along. He's good with numbers,' said Tuart affectionately. 'I can't remember naff all.'

'He knew Sun Hill's number, just like that? Any idea how?'

'From phoning about the job, I suppose.'

'The job?'

'You know, becoming a copper.' Again there was veneration in Tuart's tone. 'He rang for information – how to apply, and so forth.'

'Robbie wants to be a policeman?'

'Nothing wrong in that, is there?'

There is, thought Roach acidly, if you make up cock-and-bull stories to impress everybody. He stormed off to the interview room, shouted a question at Deacon over Lines' startled head, and went on his raging way to find Conway in the CAD room, having another go at Monroe out there in the night. He soon took the chief inspector's mind off the rest of them as he reported that their precious Mr Deacon wanted to be a police officer. That was all it was about. Now there was a glimmering of sense. This whole circus had been started off by a kid who knew the station phone number by heart: a fabrication to show what a wonderfully alert and enthusiastic crime buster he would make.

Conway said flatly: 'He's admitted it's a hoax?'

'It sticks out a –'

'Has he actually admitted it, in so many words?'

Roach slowed down. 'That he wants to be a copper, yes.'

'But not that he's made this up?'

'Oh, come on, guv, what more do you want? I just knew him and his dopey friend were a pair of bozos as soon as I set eyes on them.'

Monroe was niggling from the radio, wondering where all the headquarters' contacts had faded away to. Asked for his assessment of the current situation, he could report only that the second sweep was nearly finished, the dog handlers had come up with nothing, and the general feeling was that they were on to a loser. If there had been any supporting evidence, everyone would be keener. But basically both police officers and dogs were just chasing about in the dark.

Conway made his decision. They would finish the sweep and then pull the plug. Once that had been established with Monroe, he felt he would like a word with Mr Deacon. Or maybe rather more than just one word.

The dogs were shepherded back into their vans. Police vehicles slewed off the rough parking area they had made for themselves on the gravelly corner of Canley Fields. Monroe looked at his watch, swore under his breath, and made a number of mental calculations as he headed for the Sun Hill van.

'I notice,' said the indefatigable Reg Hollis, 'they blow the whistle just as we're getting into overtime.'

Back at Sun Hill, Conway had opted for frigid politeness rather than the scouring diatribe he had first wanted to level at Robert Deacon. Deacon would still not deny that he and his mate had seen the man and the boy; and disarmingly did not deny that he respected the police and dearly wished to become a policeman. It was not what you would call an indictable offence.

'We are grateful for your assistance,' said Conway as he personally escorted Deacon and Tuart from the interview room to the front entrance, cluttered as it was with boxes which might have come from Barton Street or might be on their way to Barton Street. 'But in the absence of any additional evidence that a crime has been committed, there's a limit to what we can do.'

'Yeah, sure.' Deacon's tired, disillusioned face reflected a disenchantment with the police and all their doings. He seemed unlikely to pursue that romantic career in uniform whose prospect had drawn him this far.

'So thanks again for coming forward,' said Conway with radiant insincerity, 'and we'll let you know if anything further comes to light.' He stuck out a hand. 'Goodbye, Mr Tuart . . . Mr Deacon.'

As they were led out, Roach said: 'We should be charging them with wasting police time.'

Conway did not want to know. Conway had reached his present rank as a result of dogged persistence and meticulous observance of the rules rather than by flair or any outstanding specialized talent. He was determined in pursuit, when the conditions and probable end of the pursuit were predictable. Loose ends were not for him. They could irritate, scratch at the fingers of your memory, for a long time. But basically you had to learn when to write a thing off. Now was well and truly the time to write off this whole shambles.

He heard two of the Sun Hill vehicles edging back into the yard below. Now came the task of sorting out the vehicles for re-allocation to the relief, and for working out which officers had been where, and for how long. Reports had to be written, all reporting nothing worthy of remembrance.

He would have been better occupied finishing off that lobster thermidor.

It was one minute past ten o'clock in the evening. Norika Datta, jotting down a note in the log, was tugged back to the console for an incoming call. As Monroe returned from Canley Fields and came in muttering angrily to Conway, she was saying in her most comforting voice: 'You're not being a nuisance at all, Mrs Butler. Really. But I'm sure there's nothing to worry about. Just a minute, let me get the details.' She reached for her pad, and jotted down an address and a brief note below it. 'Of course we will,' she said with warm reassurance. 'Just stay at home, and we'll be in touch. Goodbye, Mrs Butler.'

It had been done most soothingly; but it did not soothe Conway and Monroe. They looked down over the console at WPC Datta, recognizing trouble in the calculated calmness of her response to the caller.

Reading quietly from the notes on her pad, she said: 'Graeme Butler. Aged eight. Blond hair. Left his friend's house at seven-fifteen. Not home yet.'

Seven

In daylight a new search detail set off across Canley Fields with Monroe in charge. Chief Inspector Conway would have preferred to hover around the CAD room picking up every bit of information as it came in; but Chief Superintendent Brownlow had other ideas. He had obviously lain awake fretting about the collapse of Operation Middleman, and this morning that was his top priority. Once the chief super got an obsession it took some unsticking. By the middle of the morning the table in his portakabin had acquired a wide coating of log sheets, custody records and statement forms, with further supplies waiting in a cardboard box on the floor.

At least no crucial files had gone mysteriously missing, and the meticulous log sheets for once read more like Alastair Greig than Enid Blyton. Brownlow nodded approval; and now wanted further action.

Conway was anxious not to jump the gun on this delicate matter. From what they could deduce from the accumulation of evidence, there were very few places where Operation Middleman could possibly have leaked. Everything pointed, regrettably, to the CID. Greig had pulled Kenneth Stoller in; he and Burnside had interviewed the man; and it was Burnside who had set up the surveillance and the raid. The uniformed branch knew no details of the target until the briefing. Yet Middleman had been blown.

'Doesn't leave a lot of people in the frame, does it?' sighed Conway.

Brownlow dipped into the box for another sheet and

skimmed down it. 'It's good security to restrict information to those who need to know,' he said, *when* they need to know. But I think in the circumstances we might ask Greig to join us for a few moments, to clarify a few points.'

Brownlow was re-reading Greig's statement when the detective sergeant presented himself in the doorway of the portakabin. The chief super nodded a curt but courteous welcome, and Conway began without preamble:

'According to your account, in the course of the interview with Stoller he agreed to become an informant and offered certain information, which is recorded here.'

'Yes, sir.'

'None of this information relates directly to the premises and the suspects who were targeted in Operation Middleman.'

'No, sir.'

Brownlow leaned forward. 'Did Stoller tell you anything that wasn't recorded?'

'No, sir. That's a complete record.'

'What about informal conversations – in the corridors, or after Stoller was bailed?'

'No other information was given in the station. I wasn't with Stoller after he was bailed.'

'Was anybody?' demanded Brownlow.

Alastair Greig paused, then said reluctantly: 'Inspector Burnside gave Stoller a lift home.'

Conway looked straight at him. 'So when did *you* first learn of the target premises and suspects for Operation Middleman?'

'At the briefing. Here.'

Brownlow and Conway exchanged pessimistic glances. Sooner or later Burnside would have to be hauled in for some intensive questioning. It was not going to be pleasant. But it was not a thing to be postponed too long.

As levelly as possible Conway said: 'Is DI Burnside on the premises at the moment?'

'I believe he's out with DI Wray, sir.'

'Perhaps you'll leave a message for him to contact me,' said Brownlow, 'the moment he returns.'

The CID car sat across the road from the tube station entrance, its radio silent and its two occupants silent. Frank Burnside looked straight ahead, not wanting to share anything with Gordon Wray yet knowing he would be forced to. Everything was being taken slyly, slowly out of his hands. And he was not even sure that Wray, pretending to take his advice and aiming to take over his snout entirely for the good of the cause, was not in fact under orders to watch and listen for any little slip that would prove him a traitor.

Wray spoke at last. 'You did fix it for twelve noon?'

'You know damn well I did.'

Wray glanced at his watch. Maybe he won't show.'

'Oh, he'll show all right. He knows me well enough. But he won't like having you in on it. I can't say I like it myself.'

'Just point Stoller out to me, Frank,' said Wray patiently, 'and make sure he sees us together. Then I'll follow him down the tube, make the meeting same as you would.'

'I don't know if he'll wear it. Could be on his toes.'

'Then what – jump bail? He's a casual burglar and a druggie, not Al Capone.'

'He's my snout, and nobody else should be working him. I've never been dumped on like this, not in all my years in the job.'

'Leave it out. I've only got one paper hankie.'

'Stoller would talk to *me*. He'd have to. He owes me.'

'And then he'd come up out of the tube and swear blind you made him do a Jimmy Riddle on the live rail. And people are in the mood to believe that.'

'People?'

'Some people,' said Wray mildly. 'That's why it's better I'm the one who talks to him.'

They fell back into stiff silence again. It was another minute before Burnside saw the familiar gangling figure slouching along the opposite pavement. Grudgingly he nudged Wray in the ribs.

'Over there. The skinny git, the one who looks like if he studied hard he could be a failure.'

'Got him.'

They watched as Stoller slowed by the tube station entrance and looked furtively around. After a few seconds he spotted Burnside in the car. Burnside jerked his head to indicate Wray. Stoller looked unhappy, just as Burnside had predicted he would. There was every chance of his doing a runner. But then he averted his eyes and went into the station.

Wray got out of the car. 'Cheers, Frank. I'll shout for someone to pick me up.'

'Don't hesitate, Gordon.'

Burnside watched Wray cross the road and disappear in pursuit of Kenneth Stoller. It hurt. It got right down into his guts and twisted them. He ought to have been the one going into that station, catching up with Stoller, laying it on the line with Stoller. Stoller would talk to him. He desperately wanted to know the truth behind the other evening's fiasco; yet at the same time he was half hoping that Wray would make a mess of it.

Glumly he drove back to Sun Hill.

It would never do to show defeatism to the rest of the team. As Alastair Greig edged out of the CID cabin and along the walkway, Burnside greeted him with forced affability. 'Wotcher, Al, me old son.'

'Guv,' Greig acknowledged coolly, and added at an even lower temperature level: 'The chief super would like to see you as soon as you're back.'

It was no warmer inside the cabin. He had heard a babble of voices as he approached the door, but when he went in there was sudden silence, as if a radio speaker had been turned off. Carver, Dashwood and Viv Martella all at once seemed engrossed in paperwork, not looking at him.

Whatever the evidence still to be collected on Operation

Middleman, it looked as if the Sun Hill CID jury had already reached its verdict.

Burnside trudged grimly back along the walkway and round the corner towards Brownlow's office.

If he had been expecting something new, he was to be disappointed. He thought they had already had their post-mortem, but the chief superintendent had apparently been checking and double-checking, collecting reports and every scrap of paper the building could yield up; and all to produce the same conclusions they had already established.

After five minutes of the recital of blunders and bafflements, Burnside protested. 'We've been through all this.' Now he knew what it felt like to be the suspect in an interview room, with everything being repeated interminably until he cracked and confessed, or put one foot fatally wrong.

'I'm sorry, Frank, but we need to establish what went wrong with Middleman.'

'I know what went wrong. That slag Stoller did a number on me. Only you won't let me talk to him and clear it up.'

Conway produced a warning growl. 'Frank . . .'

'Gordon Wray can walk straight in from pulling God knows what strokes in the Drugs Squad . . . we don't know him from Adam . . . and he's given the run of the manor.'

'Inspector Burnside!' snapped Brownlow. 'We wouldn't have called you in here again if you'd cooperated fully in the first place.'

'I've got nothing to hide.'

Conway said: 'You didn't make it clear, earlier on, that your information from Stoller was an entirely private arrangement between you and him.'

'That's the way I deal with snouts. It's no secret.'

'The way you described it earlier on,' Conway persevered, 'the information came out of the interview you and DS Greig conducted with Stoller.'

'It came as a *result* of the interview. What difference does it make?'

'It means that before the briefing,' said Brownlow, 'you
78

were the only officer who knew where the raid would be.'

'Yes, but Stoller knew. Why else would we have gone?'

'But Stoller's connection, Mark Duggan, wasn't warned of the raid. The suppliers, on the other hand, seem to have been.'

Burnside had put up with this so far, but was standing no more. If he was under investigation he was entitled to the official form detailing the charges against him.

Bluntly he said: 'Form 163, if you please, sir.'

Brownlow looked uncomfortably at Conway. 'Frank, we were hoping to get this ironed out informally.'

'No Form 163,' said Burnside, 'no comment.'

In answer to Wray's call, Tosh Lines drove to the tube station and waited for the DI to emerge. Wray must have been just inside, pinching a free read of the headlines on the early edition of the evening paper, stacked up on the news-vendor's box. He came striding across the road, and Lines waited for the order to take him back to Sun Hill.

Instead, Wray said: 'Barton Street.'

Lines grimaced. Sheer necessity made regular visits to that nick inevitable, but the fewer the better, so far as most of them were concerned. As he drove he was aware of Wray covertly studying him, maybe wondering how much to trust him. Well, he could make up his own mind about that. Lines concentrated on the road.

'Kenny Stoller,' said Wray tentatively.

'What about him?'

'You and Greig and Carver pulled him.'

'Yeah.'

'Known to you before that?'

'Not me personally. He's got previous for burglary.'

'On this ground?'

'And elsewhere.'

'I've just been talking to him.'

Tosh Lines was giving nothing away. All he wanted to know was what Wray was getting him into. 'That right?'

'Didn't get anything out of him,' said Wray. 'Not from what he said, anyway. But the way he was looking at me, the way he was talking . . . he was giving off vibes, sort of saying "We both know this is bullshit, we're playing a game". Know what I mean?'

'Sure.'

'So when I was asking him if his information was kosher, and who could have blown out that operation, he was really saying "You don't need me to tell you, you're probably in it yourself".'

'Ah.'

'Something in Stoller's experience,' said Wray heavily, 'tells him a copper round here could be as bent as a corkscrew.'

Lines was unsure what sort of reply was expected to this; so made none. No further exchanges were offered until they turned into Barton Street yard and walked through to the sour, unwelcoming face of Sergeant Coles in the custody area. Wray briskly asked for interview facilities and for Mark Duggan to be brought along from his cell.

Coles made an entry in the custody record, doing it with deliberate slowness. 'You can use the interview room across there.' He did not even look up. 'And give him back in the same state as you get him. We're sensitive about that round here.'

Not before time, thought Lines dourly, remembering that Coles himself had been the one to beat up a Sun Hill prisoner on these premises. He thought it wiser, though, to keep such comments to himself.

Mark Duggan was delivered to the interview room. He had looked pretty fearsome that unforgettable evening when wielding a machete. Now he was almost cowering, shrunken in on himself, and Lines got the feeling that he was restraining himself with difficulty from looking over his shoulder. Yet there were only Wray and himself here, both sitting in front of the prisoner, and a blank wall behind him.

Wray pushed a packet of cigarettes across the table. Duggan seized it eagerly and took out a cigarette which he had a momentary, shivering difficulty in lighting.

'Right,' said Wray. 'You'll have been told that we're opposing bail on what amounts to an attempted murder charge.'

'I told you. Self defence.'

'I was on the receiving end, and it looked like attempted murder to me.'

'Self defence,' said Duggan again.

'With a machete, against an unarmed police officer?' said Lines. 'It's not on, Mark.'

'I told you, you never know who's going to come busting in and –'

'A villain trying to rip off a crack factory might go in shouting "police",' Wray conceded. 'I could be convinced, in certain circumstances.' He raised a sandy eyebrow in Lines' direction.

Tosh took the hint. 'That's a generous view, guv. But it all depends on Mark admitting he *thought* he was holding cocaine.'

Duggan shook his head despairingly.

'If he admits that,' said Wray, 'I might change my mind. And if the intended victim' – he tapped his chest – 'decides it maybe wasn't attempted murder after all . . .'

'Mark might find himself out on bail,' Tosh finished for him.

Mark Duggan looked from one to the other, incapable of deciding whether to throw himself on their mercy or keep his mouth shut. At last he muttered: 'I didn't say what you wanted back there. I'm certainly not going to say it here.'

Something in the hunted expression in his eyes, the apprehensive tilt of his head, alerted Wray and Lines at one and the same moment. Without a word Wray took a ballpoint pen from his pocket and laid it across the open end of the cigarette packet. Duggan stared for a moment. A bead of perspiration formed above his left eye and trickled down into the eyelid. After what seemed an eternity he reached

81

for the pen, scribbled on the open flap, and pushed both pen and packet hurriedly back across the table.

Wray picked up the packet and read what was scrawled inside.

Very loudly he said: 'Well, then, there's no more to be said for the moment, Mark. I can see that. But I'll be talking to you again, very shortly.'

When the custody sergeant had ungraciously taken charge of the returned prisoner and the two Sun Hill men had quit the premises, Wray said: 'All right, what was all that about, in there?'

'Never said a word.'

'You didn't have to. The whole place was awash with bloodymindedness. What's going on?'

'Thought you'd heard it all.' Lines debated how much it was reasonable to confide in this outsider. They had trouble enough already. Burnside might be stroppy half the time; but better the devil you knew than the one you weren't too sure about. 'You must have been told.'

'Cobblers. What's it all about?'

'There's a complaint against that sergeant. Terry Coles. Thumping one of our Sun Hill bodies.'

'Yes, now you mention it –'

'So what was the message?' Lines wanted his *quid pro quo*. 'What was Mark Duggan scared to say out loud?' When there was no reply, he slowed the car to a crawl so that he could lose his temper without losing the vehicle. 'Or am I in the frame and all? Look, guvnor, I'll be your bagman if that's the way the rules and regs have it. I'll run round after you because that's orders. But you treat me like a bog-roll, and you'll find I'm full of splinters.'

Wray slipped the cigarette packet from his pocket. 'All right, Tosh, keep your hair on.' He tugged back the flap as they stopped at a set of traffic lights, and held it towards Lines. Tosh looked down. The scribble read: *Can't talk in this nick.*

'Uhu.' Tosh Lines picked up the echoes. 'Of course he could be pratting us about.'

'This is a slag. He's being offered the door on an attempted murder. What'd he want to play games for?'

'Uhu.' Lines was beginning to get the outlines of the picture. It was not a very fetching work of art.

As they swung into Sun Hill yard, narrowly avoiding a skip piled high with fragments of what looked like the LIO's wall and plasterboard, Wray mused: 'I get Stoller, who thinks we're all bent. You tell me Barton Street's known for being naughty. And now' – he waved the cigarette packet – 'I get this.'

'How you feeling?'

'Eh?'

'Sounds like a good time,' said Lines, parking the car, 'to go sick.'

He had no idea where DI Wray was off to right now, but suspected it might be to do a bit of underhand reporting to Conway or even to Brownlow direct. Lines himself headed as a matter of course for the CID portakabin.

Burnside was on the phone as he entered. Lines caught only the tail-end, and only one end at that, of a mumbled conversation. 'You always said give you a bell if I was considering a move . . . sure, let's have a drink and . . . sure, get your secretary to get back to me . . .' Burnside saw Lines through the glass and put the receiver down quickly. 'Tosh! Come in here and shut the door.' When Lines was inside, he fired it like a bullet: 'Well?'

'Guv?'

'Wray. What's he been up to?'

'He's been putting himself about a bit,' said Tosh Lines uncomfortably.

'What did he get out of Stoller?'

'You'd better ask him that, hadn't you?'

Burnside was going reddish-brown in the face, in a slow wave seeping up from his throat. Only his chin, always blue in spite of careful shaving, remained its usual colour. 'You want to make your mind up, Tosh. You on my firm or not?'

'Look, I wasn't there when he talked to Stoller, was I?'

Burnside allowed himself a slow, hissing intake of breath. 'All right. What else did he do?'

'Interviewed Mark Duggan.'

'And?'

'Nothing.' Lines hesitated. 'So far as I could tell.'

Burnside's breathing seemed to be getting worse. 'You start bullshitting me, Lines, and you'll live to regret it. They haven't got the skids under me yet.'

It was Tosh's turn to lose his temper. 'All right, I'll tell you this much, and see how you like it. This whole deal smells of bent coppers. And I'm watching my back, because when that sort of diarrhoea bomb goes off, everybody gets splattered.'

He marched out of the DI's office without waiting for an answer.

PC George Garfield and WPC Suzanne Ford found Graeme Butler's body soon after lunchtime. It was not in the tangle of brambles and stunted bushes through which the men and dogs had forced a way in the hours of darkness, but in a spot so exposed that nobody would have thought of looking there. On the far side of Canley Fields, almost devoid of shrubbery but equally devoid of footpaths or anything so formal as park gates or even a public toilet, there was a tract of earth beaten hard by some rough-and-ready games of football. Wavering trails led from it where cyclists had indulged in wheelies over a sequence of bare, twisted hummocks. Years ago a shelter with wooden seats and glass partitions had been installed by an optimistic council on the recommendation of community workers and a local help-the-aged group. It now lacked all the glass and most of the slats in the wooden seats. Words, some unidentifiable and some all too clearly identifiable, had been sprayed on the peeling walls and on the shabby roof overhangs. Suggestions were made about the activities of Shirleen and Frankie. It was doubtful if anybody ever read them: the place was shabby, crumbling, and abandoned.

The motionless, slightly twisted body of the eight-year-old Graeme had been tucked neatly under one of the seats. It looked quite placid, as if the perpetrator had been concerned about his posture and comfort, and wanted to preserve the decencies.

But the boy's face was not placid. His mouth and eyes, and the marks on his neck, made it plain that he had been strangled.

Eight

Frank Burnside had not been in on the original hunt for the supposedly missing boy who had then been declared genuinely missing, and now was found again. Involved in Operation Middleman, the DI could hardly have been expected to be in two places at the same time. He was not invited to pick up the threads of the child murder inquiry. Conway and Monroe had been in on it from the start, and as the whole investigation was reactivated they seemed to have taken it into their heads to rely on DS Ted Roach so far as CID were concerned. Nor was Burnside encouraged to pick up the threads, tenuous as they might be, of the bungled Operation Middleman. It could not have been made plainer that he was under a cloud, and was destined to be kept out of any serious commitment until . . .

Well, until when?

It was six o'clock. There was surely work to be done, work that needed doing, somewhere. But not by Detective Inspector Burnside. He might as well go home. Nothing could be more demoralizing than the realization that that was precisely what they'd be happy for him to do. Go home and stay there until morning, and then come in and sit around well away from sensitive material, and wait until you were allowed a few menial jobs in the company of that rat Wray. That was how it seemed to be shaping up.

He would have to make a few more phone calls, remind one or two people of the offers they had made at one time and another, opening up jobs in private security.

It stank. All of it, it stank.

He walked morosely across the yard to his car, and was

putting the key in the door when Viv Martella leaned over the railing by the portakabin. 'Guv! Guvnor!'

'Hello, gorgeous.' He made a big effort to keep it on the usual rough, joshing level. 'Changed your mind about coming to look at my ceiling?'

She hurried down to join him, waving a slip of paper.

'Message, guv. From DI Wray.'

'Make his day.' Burnside opened the car door. 'Tell him I'm dead.'

'It's urgent, sir.' She thrust the paper at him. 'He said try at your home if we didn't catch you here. Or round the pub.'

Reluctantly Burnside straightened up and took the message slip. The name of the hospital was familiar, but not the reason for Wray wanting him round there as fast as he could make it. Too much to hope that Wray had been run over by a bus and with his dying breath wanted to pass on all his secrets.

He drove off to the hospital.

They directed him to a corridor with a sequence of private rooms. At the end, Tosh Lines was peering through a glass panel while DI Wray issued PC Melvin with terse instructions.

'You got the picture? You stick with him here until you're relieved by someone from Sun Hill. Not from anywhere else. Least of all from Barton Street. Understood?'

'Yes, guv.'

'And this is the last visit he gets until further notice.'

Melvin nodded obediently.

Wray moved to meet Burnside and took him into a recess on the corner of the corridor. 'Glad they found you, Frank.'

'What's all this in aid of?'

'Late this afternoon,' said Wray, 'Mark Duggan threw a wobbler in his cell at Barton Street. Eyes watering, snotty nose, sweating. Complained of stomach cramps. They called in the surgeon. After talking to Duggan he diagnosed heroin withdrawal, and had him brought here.'

'Never knew Duggan was on H.'

87

'No, well, he's not,' said Wray calmly. 'I put him up to it, to get him out of Barton Street.'

Burnside gave a hoarse, subdued whistle. 'And they call *me* a chancer!'

'Now he's out of the nick and away from prying ears, he's going for a deal. We drop all charges against him and his tart, Wendy.'

'And he's coming across?'

'It's like the Eurovision Song Contest. Come and have a sample.'

They went back to the door of the room. As Wray pushed it open, Burnside gave Tosh Lines a sidelong glance, and got a sheepish, half apologetic one in return. Whose side was Tosh on right now?

Mark Duggan, propped up in bed and looking as healthy as he would ever look, studied the two of them anxiously.

'Come on,' said Wray affably. 'You know Inspector Burnside. He laid a stick across you when you made that little . . . um . . . mistake.'

'I've seen the light since then, Mark.' Burnside felt an inexplicable cheerfulness welling up within him. 'I use charm these days. What you got to say?'

Mark Duggan had plenty to say. Most of it reinforced Burnside's own suspicions and guesswork. He and Wendy had indeed been expecting a delivery of coke. The customers were all lined up. And yes, Kenny Stoller had been one of them. The messenger came to the door as expected, and delivered the packet they had been waiting for. They had not immediately checked it out, because the messenger said he was not expected to collect the cash: that had been fixed by the sender. It was not a particularly unusual arrangement. Payments were often sorted out between dealers and cookers without risking receipts and prying eyes.

'So me and Wendy was getting ready to cook it into rock,' said Duggan, 'when you lot come steaming in.'

'And it wasn't the real stuff anyway.'

'We wasn't to know that.'

'Nor us,' said Burnside malevolently. 'Both of us got set up. A great joke. Or something.' He looked at Wray.

Wray said: 'Barton Street.'

'Well,' said Duggan, shifting into a more comfortable position against his pillow, 'it's well known.'

'What for?'

'There's a sergeant there doing business.'

'What sort of sergeant?' Burnside's fingernails bit into his palms. 'Uniform . . . detective?'

'Uniform. Sergeant Coles.'

'You met this Sergeant Coles?'

'Not before today. But I'd been warned. Told about him.' Momentarily Duggan did show signs of possible illness. He looked past them as if expecting a menacing face to appear beyond the glass panel.

'How did you know about him?'

'Through Kenny Stoller.'

'Stoller!' breathed Burnside.

'They look after each other, right?'

'So what happened in Barton Street?'

What had happened was that Sergeant Coles had come into the cell in the morning and woken Duggan up. He had a towel with him. 'Stand up, you slag,' he said. And when Duggan pushed himself dazedly to his feet, the sergeant said, 'You've heard of me?' And then he said, 'I don't have to say no more, do I?' He wrapped the towel round his fist, said, 'And neither do you, slag,' and punched Duggan hard in the guts.

That was it. And Burnside needed no telling that that was why Wray had found such devious means of extricating Duggan from Barton Street. Just for once you had to hand it to Wray. The two of them left the room and quickened their pace along the corridor. Melvin stayed stiffly on duty beside the door. Lines trotted to catch up with the others.

'Now I'm having Stoller,' said Burnside vengefully.

Wray shook his head. 'Now *we're* having Stoller, Frank. Who can we put on the ground?'

Burnside glanced at his watch. Greig and Carver were on

night duty. Ted Roach and Mike Dashwood would probably still be in *The Grapes*. 'And Tosh,' he said with all the old fierce gleam, 'loves the old overtime, don't you, Tosh?'

Tosh Lines sighed. 'Can I ring the wife?'

'Can you hell,' said Wray. 'This is Operation Corkscrew, and I want it watertight.'

The shadows under the block of flats were confusing. The parking area had been graced with a few strips of neon lighting. Half of these were out of order; the rest threw harsh light against the concrete pillars and the shadows of those pillars deceptively into corners, blurring against parked cars. A few gaps remained between the cars.

Through one of them slipped a kid in a bomber jacket, his hands deep in his pockets. He was making a poor show of looking casual, pretending to belong here. One of the shadows wavered towards him from behind an ageing Chevette. The two were close together for only a matter of seconds, but something changed hands and the kid scuttled away. The other shadow moved towards the exit carriageway.

Leaning against a pillar close to the stairwell, Mike Dashwood leaned over his PR.

'Go!'

A CID car accelerated out of the row of parked cars, its headlights on full beam cutting a swathe of brightness round and up the carriageway. Kenneth Stoller, trapped in the glare, tried to shield his eyes and at the same time dash for the street. Another car slid out across his path. Unable to stop, he took a dive over the bonnet, but scrambled to his feet. Greig and Lines sprang out at him and made a grab, but missed. Stoller stumbled back across the concrete flooring, heading for a grassy bank at the other end.

Burnside and Roach stepped from behind the last line of pillars, Burnside moving across at an angle so that Stoller cannoned into him. Stoller had not been ready for the impact. Burnside had. He grabbed the lapel of Stoller's jacket with his left hand, and hit him hard in the stomach with his right.

As Stoller doubled up, Ted Roach moved between him and Burnside in case the DI decided to make a meal of it. But Burnside was standing back, holding up his hands and grinning.

'He made a sudden movement,' he recited mockingly as Alastair Greig reached them, 'which caused me to believe he was about to assault me, so I struck him in self-defence.' He jerked his head at Greig. 'Write that down, Al. They believe your log sheets.'

Wray, emerging from the shadows, glared; but made no comment.

Carver and Dashwood pulled Stoller to his feet and partly supported him, partly pushed him to the nearest car. When their prey was safely in the back seat, Wray and Burnside slid in, one to either side. The car drew away into the brighter lighting of the streets. The glow shifting erratically across Kenneth Stoller's face did not show him at his best.

Burnside said: 'You've upset me, Kenny.'

'You dropped Mr Burnside right in it, didn't you?' intoned Wray.

'You grassed Mark Duggan up to me, and then you slipped the wink to Terry Coles at Barton Street, and he warned the suppliers off. That's how it was, right? Then they sold Duggan a dummy, and we steamed in and looked like a pack of plonkers.'

Still hugging his stomach, Stoller gasped: 'I'm entitled to a lawyer.'

'You won't get a lawyer to jump on board a moving vehicle, Kenny. Legal aid doesn't pay enough.'

'Of course,' said Wray, 'once we get to the station we'll get you a brief.'

Burnside looked at the back of the driver's neck. 'What d'you reckon to the traffic tonight, Jim?'

Carver slowed for a crossing, and stayed slow once he had cleared it. 'Diabolical. Could take hours.'

'Still, young Kenny knows what he's entitled to.'

Stoller looked apprehensively from one of them to the other.

Wray said: 'We all know what he's entitled to. He's entitled to be done for possession, dealing in controlled substances . . .'

'He's broken his bail conditions, so he's entitled to be remanded in custody . . .'

'And conspiracy to pervert the course of justice, he's entitled to be done for that.'

'What will a brief tell him?'

'Tell him to keep his mouth shut. "See you in Brixton jail in a couple of months' time."'

They stared at Stoller. He tried now to evade their glances, but found himself confronted by Dashwood, leaning back over the front seat and appraising him inquisitively. His head sank between his hands and he hunched forward.

'Or,' said Wray reflectively over Stoller's head to Burnside, 'the poor little sod could do without what he's entitled to, and go home. *If* . . .' He let it hang on the air.

There was no sign of a traffic jam, but Jimmy Carver was driving even more slowly.

'After what happened last time,' said Burnside, 'I don't see how we could trust him. Not very reliable, our Kenny.'

Stoller tried to take quick glances at them without raising his head more than a couple of inches.

'Oh, we'd have to be very sure this time,' Wray agreed. 'This time Kenny will have to sing for his supper. He'll have to get up in front of an audience – and perform. And it'll have to be a very, very convincing performance.'

It was not just Sun Hill that was being rebuilt. Apparently the reconstruction fever had also bitten British Rail, and the railway station approach boasted ten times as many scaffolding poles, plank walkways, and miles of cable as the police station. Alastair Greig and Tosh Lines had picked their way expertly over a dozen hazards, and finally reached the comparative tranquillity of a temporarily unused

office overlooking the concourse and four of the main platforms. Their angle on the space before the barriers was
limited, but took in all the seats that remained intact
within the building operations. It would be bad luck if
their quarry chose somewhere else for the rendezvous. It
would be even worse luck for Kenny Stoller if he had mis-
led them.

On the dusty table Greig had laid out binoculars, his PR,
a radio receiver and headphones, and a small speaker. Lines
busied himself opening a holdall and extracting a collapsible
tripod and camera.

Greig studied him sceptically. There was always something
lumbering and unskilled about Tosh's movements, like those
of a plump actor impersonating a lovable but floundering
teddy bear. 'You know what you're doing with that thing?'
Greig ducked as a leg of the tripod swung loose and threatened to impale him.

'Been on a course, haven't I?' said Lines defensively.

'Well, don't point it at me. They make me nervous.'

He was reaching for the binoculars when Wray's voice
crackled in the PR. 'Corkscrew Two from Corkscrew One,
receiving?'

Lines was closest to the receiver. 'Corkscrew Two, go
ahead, guv.'

'Are you in position?'

'In position, just setting up equipment.'

'Report as soon as you're active. We don't know exactly
when this thing's going down.'

'Or even if,' said Lines softly as he turned away from
the table.

Greig scanned the concourse with the glasses. A suburban
train spilled a few clusters of passengers on to the platform.
They bunched together at the barrier, fussed impatiently
through, and spread out in three different directions towards
exits and the tube line. It was difficult from this angle to pick
out any individual face.

'Do you think he'll show?' he muttered.

'If I were Terry Coles,' said Lines, 'I'd be here already, sussing the plot out.'

It was not a comforting thought.

Greig edged into the extreme corner of the window. From here he could just see the back of a plain van parked beside two large parcel trolleys in the slip road beyond the end platform. It was easy to visualize Burnside and Wray tucked clumsily in there, without the facilities or the larger viewing windows of the Sun Hill van. If the Sun Hill vehicle itself had been used, it was reasonable to guess that Coles would have spotted it within a matter of seconds.

And somewhere out there, approaching the station entrance, Dashwood was due just about now. He, too, would be in a hired car.

At the very instant Greig looked at his watch, Dashwood's voice came through. 'Corkscrew Three to Corkscrew Two. Checking transmission.'

'Receiving, Mike. Go ahead.'

He heard the voices clearly. Dashwood was saying, 'Give me a fiver,' and answering Stoller's startled yelp with, 'Make it look like a minicab, got it?' Then he went on in a measured rhythm: 'Mary had a little pig, she couldn't stop it grunting . . .'

'You what?'

Stoller had been satisfactorily wired up. Both his own voice and Dashwood's were sharp and intelligible. After a moment they separated as Stoller came somewhere into the station below, and Dashwood drove off round the block.

Dashwood confirmed it. 'Jailbait is on the plot.'

Greig jacked the radio receiver into a cassette recorder and pushed them to one end of the table. He slipped headphones over his ears, and manoeuvred the binoculars with one hand. Less deftly, Lines adjusted the camcorder on its tripod. They waited; peered down; cursed when another trainload filled the concourse with a swaying wave of people. A man came and sat on one of the seats. Then an elderly couple laden with cases and plastic shopping bags claimed another in its entirety. One or two more like that, and Stoller would have nowhere to sit, and there was no telling how far out of range he might be led.

He was supposed to establish his presence by going to look at the departures board. He ought by now to have got through the passage between boarded-up sections of the building and be out on the concourse. Greig breathed an impolite invitation to him to get a move on.

At last Stoller was there, insinuating himself into a handful of other people staring up at the departure times.

'Corkscrew One from Corkscrew Two. Jailbait in target area.'

'Understood,' said Wray.

Stoller sauntered towards a seat but did not sit down. Greig hesitated, wanting to keep an eye on him but also needing to sweep the concourse for a first glimpse of their next visitor. He panned to and fro; then froze. A man had come out of the half-concealed toilets below the bridge leading to further platforms. He glanced up at the clock.

It was Coles, all right. He looked less domineering, out of uniform and shrouded in a dark overcoat, but there was no mistaking that loping, rapacious walk of his.

'Corkscrew One. Jailer is on the plot.'

Now Coles was approaching the departures board. He studied it innocently enough, then looked around. It was a good act: bored, aimless, filling in time until his train was due. Until he spotted Stoller. Unhurriedly he drifted towards him. Equally unhurried, the two of them moved out of vision.

'Hell,' moaned Lines. He stooped over the camcorder as if to drag the two men bodily back into shot. He located them again, on the extreme end of a seat tucked away near the buffet. 'Give us sound, Al – it's easier to pick up the moves.'

Greig put down his binoculars and fiddled with the speaker until the sound of distant conversation came surging up.

First it was Stoller mumbling. 'Y'see, Tel, what I had to do . . . only under pressure, Tel, like . . .'

'You offering me information, or what?' growled Coles.

'Come on, Tel, you got to help us out.'

'I'm a police officer, I don't owe you any favours.'

'Look, I got Burnside on my back, and I got this geezer Wray . . .'

'I don't know why you're talking to me about it.'

Coles sounded very stiff and correct. Greig and Lines exchanged a fleeting glance, dismayed. Coles must have guessed there was a wire.

Even in their own ears Stoller's answering whine sounded hideously unconvincing. If Coles has sussed him, it must sound even more ridiculous down there. 'Sun Hill CID, they're gonna throw the book at me, Tel. They'll have me in the frame for every unsolved crime on the manor.'

'Tough tit.'

'Look, with that sort of pressure, if you don't do something for me I'll have to grass you up.'

'You're talking rubbish,' said Coles levelly. 'Nothing to do with me.'

It was blown. Despondently the two in the observation post knew the whole thing was blown again. Coles was on to it and playing it dead straight.

Stoller must have sensed it too, and was getting desperate. And clumsy. His voice squeaked half an octave higher. 'Look, I told you about the raid on Duggan's place, yeah? And you dealt with it, you put the word in. I mean, that's what you did, innit, Tel?'

Coles got to his feet. Lines kept the camcorder on him, but without much hope of any good result now.

'Don't you threaten me!' Coles spoke loudly and clearly, as if to make sure the message was well and truly recorded.

Then, as Lines zoomed in the camcorder, he seized on a dramatic, if slightly fuzzy, picture. Coles, stooping over Stoller, had tossed a Stanley knife into his lap. Stoller instinctively picked it up and stared at it. 'What the . . .?' Before he could make a move, Coles had whipped a baton from beneath his coat and was beating him about the head.

'Corkscrew One,' yelled Lines. 'Go, go, go!'

As Coles went on bashing Stoller, hammering him down to the ground while people backed away screaming, the Sun Hill CID team charged out of the van and dashed towards the scene. By the time they reached him, Coles was twisting Stoller's arm behind his back, and with the free hand displaying his warrant card.

'Police officer, in the course of his duties –'

'Get off him, Coles,' shouted Ted Roach. 'You're nicked.'

Jimmy Carver hauled Coles away from Stoller, who collapsed against the end of a luggage trolley. Ted Roach bent over him while Wray hurried up to the observation post, and Burnside confronted the defiant, sneering sergeant.

'This is bollocks,' said Coles. 'This slag here tried to set me up, and when it didn't work he pulled a blade on me. Look!' He thrust his foot towards the knife lying close to Stoller's hip.

Burnside shook his head. 'We had him wired, dumbo.'

'Yeah, well, you listen to your wire, Burnside, and see what it gives you. Sod all.'

The sergeant's brutal confidence shook them all. There was every sign of this being another operation that had gone bent on them.

Ted Roach looked up from Stoller. 'This is an ambulance job.'

'Unreasonable force?' suggested Burnside. It was a pretty thin straw to grasp.

Coles snorted.

Wray appeared at Burnside's elbow. 'We got it taped, Coles. I just got confirmation.'

'Oh, leave it out. I never said nothing. I know the business, remember?'

'Not audio tape,' said Wray softly. 'Video. We got you planting the Stanley knife, we got you committing an unprovoked assault.'

Coles, numb, let the warrant card slip through his fingers. Burnside picked it up, and for a moment there seemed a danger of him smacking Coles full across the face with it. Then, with a gust of a satisfied sigh, he said:

'You're dead, Terry.'

They stayed on longer than usual in the pub that night, celebrating victory. Even the usually dour, self-sufficient Greig looked in convivial mood, still marvelling at the near catastrophe when they thought they had lost out.

'Here you are, Tosh.' Mike Dashwood handed Lines a brimming pint. 'Coolness under fire, eh? The Kate Adie of Sun Hill!'

'Hang about . . .'

'Funny, I always had you down as an old-fashioned copper. Didn't realize you'd mastered the new technology.'

Lines shrugged. Somehow he was not so euphoric as the rest of them. There was still a lingering smell – the smell of corruption. They were used to that in lots of walks of life. But this had been within their own ranks. 'It's not the technology. It's anticipation.' He stared morosely into his beer. 'I mean, I thought, in Terry Coles's position, what would I do? And I found I was half expecting it.' It was a sobering thought. He tried to drown it by setting out to get less sober.

Burnside, at a table with Wray, waved a twenty-pound note expansively. 'Here, Mike, bung another Shakespeare in the kitty before you sit down.'

'Right you are, guv.'

There was a muffled cheer from the direction of the bar.

Burnside, full of satisfaction, looked tolerantly at Wray. He wasn't actually going to rub it in, but he could afford at any rate a tasty morsel of a gloat. 'They're a good bunch of lads on my firm, Gordon. Great *esprit de corps*.'

'Definitely the team to have behind you in a crisis,' Wray agreed.

'I'll drink to that.'

'Still,' said Wray very quietly, so that no one else could

overhear, 'I'd prefer to have kept out of the crisis in the first place.'

Burnside detected a sour note. 'Eh?'

'As the Duke of Wellington remarked after Waterloo.'

'Wrong station, Gordon.'

'Very sharp, Frank. He said it was a damned close run thing. Like today. Not the way I normally fancy doing things – cutting corners, getting your chestnuts out of the fire just before they go off bang.'

'Yeah, well, we're all different.' There was no way Burnside was going to feel less than cheerful right now. 'I mean,' he grinned, 'what we do at Sun Hill's not your problem from now on, Gordon.'

Wray pursed his lips and turned his glass unnecessarily round three times clockwise, then once anti-clockwise. 'Can I tell you something in confidence?'

'Goes without saying.'

'I've got my promotion. DCI.'

'Well, I'm glad to hear that, Gordon.' Burnside suppressed a twinge of envy, but could not suppress one gentle prod: 'Hope I don't have to wait till I'm your age.'

'I'll be moving out of the Drug Squad. Got a month's leave, and then back to divisional duties.'

'Nice work. A month lying in the sun on the Costa del Crime?'

'Skiing, actually.'

People could break a leg skiing, thought Burnside. Or break a neck. But he had already got one dig in, and was in too good a humour to say this one crudely out loud.

'Any idea whereabouts you'll be when you get back?'

Wray lowered his voice even further. 'Sun Hill, Frank.' He smiled. 'I'm your new guvnor.'

Nine

Two weeks gone, and still there had been no lead on Graeme Butler's killing. Out on the beat, checking on an illegally parked car with dubious number-plates or on a punch-up between so-called football fans who wouldn't have known a penalty from a knee in the groin, June Ackland, Norika Datta, Steve Loxton and all the rest of them were subjected day in, day out, to the sneers of those they cautioned or arrested. Fine way for the overpaid fuzz to spend the day, wasn't it? Parking tickets and easy round-ups of piss-artists, instead of finding the filthy swine who had strangled a little boy, and who'd probably do it again, and get away with it again. Choking back the replies took a lot of self-discipline. Choking the bastard who had done it would have been a lot more pleasurable.

Chief Inspector Derek Conway could regard the murder only as something so kinky as to be beyond belief. It was a matter of methodically tracking down the culprit, delivering him to the courts, and hoping he got shut away, before getting on to the next job in hand. Perversities of that kind did not happen to people like the Conways: he had one son at university, one at the local comprehensive, and an eight-year-old daughter who would not be allowed to wander off on her own – or want to. That was what sensible family life was about.

Inspector Andrew Monroe had been married for twenty years, found nothing wrong with his marriage, and had made sure that nothing would ever go wrong with his two teenage daughters. As a policeman he deplored both major and petty crimes because they were what he had been trained to deplore. It was his job to wrap up loose ends and be done with them. Any talk of psychological problems and the need to understand and try to rehabilitate perverts was beyond him. He and his chief inspector might differ in their methods and general approach; but they agreed in the necessity for quick action and a quick write-off.

It couldn't happen to us: that was their basic, cut-and-dried self-assurance. And probably it couldn't.

Sergeant Alec Peters was a grandfather and complacently proud of it. Sergeant Bob Cryer had two sons, one of whom had been involved in a death by dangerous driving two years back. It still rankled. Cryer loved both boys, yet grew bitter about the one who had let him down, let his standards down, turned out to be someone you couldn't talk about, let alone boast about. Yet he resented any rumour or sour hint about the boy; and could only be thankful that, whatever might have happened in recent years, the early childhood years had not been stained by anything as putrid as this.

Tosh Lines sometimes despaired over his five kids. Not because of the kids themselves, but because of his own ineptitude. He was always in debt, never able to give them everything he wanted to give. Yet they loved him. Whenever he went home and they swarmed over him and tugged his straggly moustache and weighed down on his knees and asked him for a story – any old story – he could feel, almost smell, that they loved him. Just the way he loved them: he let his wife and kids down over and over again, yet loved them. And the thought of anyone capable of twisting the neck of any kid like that, turned his stomach and made him yearn to do some twisting of his own . . . and making it last, keeping it on until the evil sod was screaming for mercy, and got none.

As for Brownlow, the chief super had issued orders in his usual booming way, demanding immediate results and saying that this was top priority: mainly because he was being asked angry questions on the golf course by the local mayor and the Deacon of his Masonic Lodge, whose building firm was worried about a possible threat to property values in what might become an area of ill repute. It was no good assuring them and the local evening rag that investigations were now formally in the hands of the Area Major Incident Pool. When the inquiry had been concluded, successfully or otherwise, and those AMIP officers had gone, the cloud of dishonour would still hang over the station: this expensive new station where they were all so pampered and comfortable now, and all so incapable of using their smart modern facilities to catch a child killer. To be honest, Brownlow's main concern at the moment was connected more with those new buildings themselves than with the ongoing problem of the murder. The glamorous public relations exercise of a ceremonial reopening of Sun Hill station was much more his cup of tea.

The renovations had in fact not been entirely completed. One or two offices were still choked with files and boxes recovered from portakabins but not yet accommodated in new cupboards with their glossy doors and magnetic catches. The truth of the matter was that the contractors were running late. But a reopening date had been announced weeks ago, and invitations issued to local dignitaries. The celebrations would have to go ahead.

Brownlow posed for a photographer on the steps of the station. Then he was asked to pose for another one next to the scaffolding which really ought not to have been there any longer. Indoors, Conway divided his time between checking on the cleanliness of the lavatories and the canteen tables, and disrupting work in the CAD room by repeatedly asking for further news on a follow-up in the boy's killing.

The assistance of Detective Chief Inspector Wray and Detective Constable Lines had been requested by the senior AMIP officer because of local contacts with which they might be more familiar. One after another, suspects had been discreetly checked, questioned, and eliminated. The latest was a school caretaker who had known the dead boy and about whom there had been one or two rumours, lingering from a previous job. Gradually it emerged that Graeme Butler had liked talking to the man and had been particularly fond of his dog. And then that the boy had called on him only half an hour before he went missing.

It looked hopeful. Using the dog as bait, with the excuse of taking it for its evening walk on Canley Fields, the caretaker could have lured Graeme along as well. Conway waited impatiently for the pay-off.

When it came it was not just a disappointment but a near-tragedy. According to the caretaker it was Graeme who had done the asking, suggesting a walk with the dog. And the man wasn't going to risk it, knowing what spiteful innuendoes there would be. But if only he had agreed . . .

If he had gone along with Graeme and they had been seen, there was little doubt what gossip and repercussions there would have been. But if he had gone along, then Graeme Butler would not now be dead.

Conway resumed his inspection of the premises.

The mayor and a number of councillors arrived, including the inevitable troublemaker who wasted no time before asking in a sour tone how investigations were proceeding into the appalling murder on their very doorstep. Brownlow hurriedly made his speech of welcome rather earlier than he had intended, and to forestall any further hostile questions invited the mayor to cut the blue velvet ribbon stretched across the front desk. They then set out on a conducted tour of the new premises. Sergeant Penny looked smart but apparently inactive in the clinically immaculate custody area. The cells were clean and sweet-smelling. Prisoners were still being processed at Barton Street until Sun Hill became fully operational again at midnight; but the visitors did not fully grasp this, and would carry away with them an impression of easy-going life in the police force. In the refurbished CAD room they looked either politely impressed by the new electronic wall charts and VDU consoles, or silently critical on behalf of the taxpayer.

It was unfortunate that as they crossed the front office

103

again on their way to the stairs and Brownlow's office for refreshments, the smoothness of the proceedings should be interrupted by a sudden yelling and struggling on the front steps. A red-faced, middle-aged man with the eruptive nose of a liquor addict was trying to fight his way in while PC Garfield, on sentry duty to keep the ceremonial reopening private, struggled to restrain him.

'I seen murder. Let me in, you've got to –'

'If you could just calm down and wait a few minutes until the –'

'I've seen the body. Murder, I tell you.'

The mayor looked at Chief Inspector Conway, wondering what to expect. A teetotal councillor wrinkled his nose at the sight of the bleary, drunken creature flailing his arms and trying to lumber past Garfield and through the entrance doors.

'I've seen it – seen the body!'

Conway skirted the group of visitors and strode out on to the steps. It was his duty to impress the attentive audience with his firmness and calmness.

'All right, sir, easy does it.'

The man took a step towards him, one arm still flailing to push Garfield out of the way. His waving fist caught Conway full on the nose. Blood began to trickle down over his lip.

'Murder! Aren't you going to listen?'

Brownlow urged his guests briskly away from the front office towards the stairs and his office, where drinks and food were waiting. Two hired waitresses circulated with wine bottles, refilling glasses. The teetotal councillor, who was also a vegetarian, looked askance at the quantity of wine being poured and at the ham cornets and twists of smoked salmon. The chairman of local Rotarians and a number of others showed less concern, making the most of what was on offer. It wasn't every day you got a free lunch of this quality in a police station.

From time to time there was a faint shout from below. Everyone politely pretended not to notice. It must be all

104

in the day's routine. But there would be some sniggers and arch surmises afterwards.

Sergeants Cryer and Penny pushed the struggling man on to a bench in the custody area and held him there, even though it meant spoiling the still virgin surface of the bench and adding a sour smell of stale alcohol and staler clothes to the fragrance of the atmosphere.

'You don't listen to me. You're not listening.'

'Just calm down,' yelled Bob Cryer, 'and then we'll listen.' He slackened his grip as the man sagged back a few inches. 'Right. What's your problem?'

'He's a scumbag wino,' said Tom Penny, 'that's his problem.'

'Your name?' said Cryer patiently.

'Hillman. Stanley Hillman. But what's that got to do with it? I seen murder . . . a body . . . I keep trying to tell you . . .'

'Where?'

'There! Where d'you think? Where else do I go?'

'How should we know?'

'By the old factory. Where we all go. You know. And that's where it is, the body.'

'One of your mates?' No great loss, thought Cryer.

Hillman was dissolving into maudlin sobs. His face dropped into his hands. 'A kid.' It came out muffled and tearful. 'She . . . she's in a sack. I opened it, and she's in there. I . . . saw her hair.'

Bob Cryer felt cold prickles going down his spine. Hillman was drunk, or slurring his way out of the last bout of drunkenness. Drunk, confused, seeing things. But there was something disconcerting there.

Another child murder? They could do without that. But the story had to be followed up.

The factory was not difficult to identify. Winos and meths drinkers often congregated in the shelter of the derelict factory in Gilfillan Road. Nobody was likely to interrupt them or make complaints about their smells and habits. Few cared to walk near the shaky walls of the old building, and the lumpy ground surrounding it was too littered with rusty cans, chains, jagged fragments of corrugated iron and other unidentifiable bits of metal to offer a pleasant stroll to even the most adventurous courting couples.

The call went out for Sierra One to investigate the reported sighting of a body in a plastic sack.

June Ackland received the message with marked lack of enthusiasm. No indication had been given as to how long the body might have been in the sack. She could only hope that it was all a false alarm.

Tony Stamp was equally disapproving as he parked the area car at the edge of the waste ground. There had once been an approach lane from ornamental gates to the factory, but the gates had gone long ago and the surface of the lane had disappeared under invading weeds and a luxuriant crop of broken bottles. There was no way of driving closer. The two of them had to get out and stumble over the mantraps of the pitted earth.

Figures stirred as they approached. There must have been half a dozen men there, sprawling or sitting with their arms round their knees, occasionally groping for a can or bottle and moaning when it was found to be empty. Twenty yards beyond the group was a heap of builders' rubble, tipped at random, and plastic sacks twitching in the wind or held down by the weight inside. At the sight of the police officers drawing near, two of the men set up a jeering chant which was probably obscene, but so disjointed that the words were incomprehensible.

Another car circled the far side of the waste ground and turned to park behind Stamp's. Dave Quinnan stumbled across the obstacle course to join them. The two men made their way to the scattering of plastic sacks and began prodding them, opening the doubtful ones and peering in. It was the tenth which brought Tony Stamp to a halt. After a moment he straightened up and beckoned June Ackland to join him.

106

She looked reluctantly into the neck of the sack. Then, fighting back her nausea, she spoke into her radio.

'Sierra Oscar from 643, receiving . . . over . . .?'

The waste ground was soon fringed by police vehicles. The immediate area in which the body had been found was screened off, and a police photographer went inside, watched with bleary interest by the winos. Ted Roach arrived, finding the answer to his first question in Lines' set, livid face.

It was another one, all right: a young girl, aged about nine. Even before the confirmation of a post mortem it was not difficult to tell that she had been strangled. She could not have been dead very long. Surely, in broad daylight, somebody must have seen something?

Questioning of the wine-sodden men began at once, before they could take fright and disappear. But they had nothing to offer. Things were thrown away all the time. This waste ground was a free dump for anybody and everybody. Of course they often rooted through the sacks themselves, to see if there was anything worth having. How else would Hillman have come across the corpse? But as to who put it there, and when, none of them had anything useful to contribute. They offered a strange catalogue of passing vehicles, including one drawn by two tigers, and one driven by a large woolly dog in a red jacket. Looking on the wine when it was red seemed to have had a remarkable effect on their vision. Questioned in one of the unblemished new interview rooms at Sun Hill, Hillman had little more to offer. He was obviously genuinely shocked; and obviously wished he had never started poking through those sacks.

The mortuary van added itself to the vehicles in Gilfillan Road.

But who was the victim?

It took less than an hour of ringing round the local schools and then visiting one to establish that. Her name was Jennie Price. She had been missing from class that morning, but the headmistress had not been alarmed: notification was

107

not automatically expected on the first day of absence. If she had been ill, either she would have brought a letter the next day or her mother would have telephoned. They were that sort of family. Some girls did play truant and the parents had to be chased up. But Jennie Price was a hard-working, conscientious girl with devoted, conscientious parents.

Somebody had to go and break the news to those parents. And one of them would have to come and identify the body.

It was beginning to look as if Sun Hill might be contaminated by what every man and woman there most hated and feared – a serial murderer on their ground.

Ten

Whatever neatness had been imposed on certain rooms in the renovated Sun Hill, a lot of it now had to be disturbed to accommodate the newly established incident room and its hasty assembly of chairs, tables and filing cabinets. The Area Major Incident Pool had shifted from Barton Street overnight, and was in process of expanding. The search had been serious enough before. Now it was acute. Every query, every shred of evidence and the most confused of hints from the public, school staff, parents of children, passers-by, had to be recorded and sieved and picked over time after time. A battery of phones had been installed. There would be at least a hundred meaningless calls a day; but each one would have to be followed up to make sure whether, in the middle of all the vagueness and attention-grabbing claptrap, there might not be something meaningful. Phones, interviews, references and cross-references to Cathy Marshall's card indexes: it all had to be checked and double-checked.

There must not be another killing.

DI Burnside led DS Roach purposefully along the corridor past the incident room, on their way to the office set aside for Detective Superintendent Jack Meadows of AMIP. Roach was hushed and uncommunicative for once. He had never expected to be put in charge of the Action Book for an investigation of this kind, and was not sure he was up to it. Or, rather, he was sure that in his own way he was up to it, but not sure of how he would be helped or hampered by the doubts and reservations of other folk in the operation. Burnside had hinted that Alastair Greig, so often the blue-eyed boy of Sun Hill CID, had neither the experience nor the nous. What was needed was an experienced, think-ing detective. Greig thought; but in a straight line. It was more than just being an office manager. There would be a thousand scraps of information flying about in the breeze, and just one could prove important. Burnside had made it flatteringly clear that he would back Roach against Greig to spot such a fragment.

'Give you a chance to prove a thing or two, as well,' he commented as they reached Meadows' door.

'Such as?'

'Ted Roach can't handle responsibility, can he?' Burnside knocked at the door. 'Show 'em different.'

Roach tensed as they went in to meet the superintendent's thin smile, which failed to conceal the shrewd appraisal behind it.

Meadows was a lean man with high cheekbones, a receding hairline, and the faint remains of a Brummie accent. His jacket was casually unbuttoned, but it was a stylishly tailored jacket. His blue and deep purple tie made no pretensions to be an old school or college one; but it was silk, and neatly knotted. He looked more like a strict, tight-lipped bank manager than a CID superintendent.

He wasted no time in formalities or matey chat. Again like a bank manager, he was not concerned with putting people at their ease. 'Ever run an incident room before, Ted?'

'No, sir. But I've been involved in plenty. I'm sure I can do a good job.'

'You struck me as being a bit uptight yesterday, after you'd informed the mother.'

Getting uptight when a kid had been murdered struck Roach as being a normal reaction. It was years since his marriage had broken up, and there had never been any children of his own to worry about. But every instinct in him cried out painfully when it was a matter of child abuse and, most of all, child murder. You never got so tough as to be able to brush that sort of thing aside; or to be indifferent when it came to telling the young mother the lousy, brutal truth.

As if reading his thoughts, Meadows said: 'I want plenty of passion in this affair, Ted. And zeal. But I don't want personal emotions getting in the way. Clarity of thought, okay? Basically you get seventy-two hours to catch a murderer before the trail goes cold. After that you're down to the long hard grind – and a hell of a lot of luck. I'd prefer to catch this man now.' The phone rang, and after he had answered it there was a grim, resentful look in his stony grey eyes. The call had not brought a fresh bit of news to make the story better or worse, but the notification that the expected press conference had to be held right now in the incident room. It was not a cheering prospect. They all knew from bitter experience how their statements would be twisted by reporters eager for a sickening story to titillate the appetites of their ghoulish readers. All in the public interest, of course.

Chief Superintendent Brownlow was talking to Conway, unsure whether to add his authority and platitudinous statements to the conference or to steer well clear of it, as Ted Roach hurried past. It was typical of Brownlow, taken aback by the speed of events and by the virtual seizure of Sun Hill staff and facilities by AMIP, to pick fretfully and demoralizingly on one of his own people. 'An unfamiliar role for you, Ted.'

Roach paused and raised a ragged ginger eyebrow. 'I think I've got something to offer, sir.'

Brownlow nodded non-committally.

The buzz and activity of the room hit Roach like some kind of numbing nerve gas. Three phones were clamouring at once, someone was tapping a computer keyboard to produce a dance of flickering figures, and a man Roach did not recognize was carefully driving coloured pins into a large street map on the wall. Come to that, he hardly recognized anybody. Trying to look efficient and in control of events, he went to the one unoccupied desk in the room, close to the board holding the map. A book lay on the desk, its light-blue card cover boldly lettered with a dark-red marker pen. The title was blunt and specific:

111

'Welcome aboard,' said a quiet voice at his elbow.

It was Cathy Marshall. Roach was relieved to find a friendly face. For a chilling moment or two he had thought that he must be in a Sun Hill minority of one. At least with Cathy on the spot there was little danger of information getting disjointed and untraceable. He sat down and opened the book at its first page, still blank, though a scribbled note giving two names and telephone numbers had been slipped immediately inside. He turned his attention to them and surreptitiously sized up the other occupants of the room. At least this was less gruelling than having to face up to a press conference.

The journalists and photographers crowded into Sun Hill canteen. At the last moment Brownlow had decided there were more pressing matters to be attended to, and left Meadows to cope with the onslaught.

Meadows adopted a steady, deadpan drone for delivering his opening statement. He would have been rather good at addressing an annual meeting of building society shareholders.

'A decision has been made at Command level to combine the investigation into the murder of Graeme Butler with that into the murder of Jennie Price. The incident room here at Sun Hill, staffed by members of the Area Major Incident Pool under my direction, will be conducting the combined investigation.'

A seasoned middle-aged journalist with steel-rimmed glasses and a dog-eared notebook was ahead of his colleagues in asking the obvious question. 'Presumably this means you believe both children were victims of the same killer?'

'That is a possibility we are not ruling out,' said Meadows guardedly.

A local radio reporter with an open-reel recorder on his
112

knee held up a microphone. 'Do you have any evidence at all so far?'

'The forensic situation is looking quite promising.'

'So an early arrest is expected?'

'We are here to do a job: to catch the person who murdered Jennie Price. Obviously we intend that to be sooner rather than later.'

Several voices tripped over one another, and questions came at Meadows in scattered splinters.

'If she never arrived at school, why –'

'Do you know if anyone saw her and if –'

'Is anyone already helping you with your inquiries?'

'Who reported the – '

In a calm, measured way Meadows recited: 'Jennie Price left her home in Leeworthy Road at eight-forty-five yesterday morning to walk to St Eunice's junior school in Penrice Street. She never arrived. Her body was found some three hours later beside Gilfillan Road, tucked into a plastic sack. She was wearing a grey skirt and blue St Eunice's blouse. We would appeal to anyone who thinks they may have seen Jennie yesterday morning to come forward. All such information will be channelled through our incident room and most carefully analysed.'

'You say Gilfillan Road. Can you give us any more details of exactly where?'

Meadows summed the facts up briefly. He was an expert at this, knowing how much the press expected and how little he could expect to get away with. He kept it matter-of-fact and impersonal, as if they were discussing a minor alteration in a one-way traffic system. When he had finished there were a few more sputters of probing speculation, not all of it friendly.

'In view of the time that's gone by since Graeme Butler's murder, without any hint of an arrest, do you think you have any better chance –'

'Mr Meadows, if I might just –'

'That's all I have for the moment, ladies and gentlemen.

We'll keep you informed the moment we have anything to offer.'

'Just one more point –'

'I'm afraid that that is all,' said Meadows implacably, 'for the moment.'

He made his escape to his office. Brownlow, as if waiting for the signal, appeared with a businesslike thrust of the head, displaying his willingness to take personal charge of everything when the basic work had been done, or make a resounding announcement when there was something to announce. At the same time Burnside came round the corner, quickening his pace to get there first. He had started speaking to Meadows before, with a bob of the head, he pretended to become aware of the chief super's presence.

'I'm off to see the parents then, guv.'

'Right. Use your gumption, Frank. If you think it'll help, bring them in.' Meadows diplomatically included Brownlow in the conversation. 'Let them see we're pulling out all the stops, you know.'

'Good thinking.'

'One thing, guv,' said Burnside. 'We're a bit short of WDCs.'

'A WPC, then.' Meadows turned again to Brownlow. 'Can you help us there, sir?'

Brownlow saw no good reason why he should not put on an immediate display of decisiveness. 'Absolutely. Take Ackland, Frank.'

'Thanks, sir. A great help.'

Burnside left before there were any changes of mind or clashes with Conway or Monroe, who would undoubtedly resent not having been consulted.

June Ackland sat silently beside Burnside as he drove towards the Prices' address. Finding the girl's body dumped in that black plastic sack had been bad enough. Meeting the parents could be a lot worse. You didn't make light conversation before facing up to that sort of ordeal.

114

Burnside was doing a few sums in his head and coming up with no answers. Meadows might make glib generalizations to the press about forensic evidence, but the reality was less helpful. Two dog hairs, one white and one black, and a single fingerprint on the sack: it was not a lot to go on, unless the fingerprint came up smelling of roses. Even then it was going to be a long and probably unrewarding process of elimination. Every known pervert on the manor would have to be wheeled in, fingerprinted, and questioned. Dashwood and Lines were already drearily working their way through all the old faithfuls on one of Cathy Marshall's lists. Odds against the guilt of any name on that list were dispiriting. Child molesters rarely turned into child killers. Though maybe this time some twisted perve had changed his habits, escalated a bit. It could not be ruled out. Damn it, *somebody* had put the kid in that sack. And somebody had strangled Graeme Butler, and the patterns were all too similar, the neighbourhoods not too close but not too far apart: surely not the work of a stranger, passing through and killing at random.

Yet every theory had to make allowance for it turning out to be just that. Nothing was predictable; easy solutions were thin on the ground.

The Prices' home in Leeworthy Road was one of a long terrace whose drab uniformity had been broken up in recent years by the addition of modern windows, pert little porches, and the out-thrust of a loft conversion. Some houses had narrow rectangles of paving stones or concrete behind low front walls. Others had been graced by tiny flowerbeds set into the paving, or by clusters of ornamental pseudo-Grecian urns. In other neighbourhoods the urns would have been smashed by hooligans long ago; but not here. This was one of the more respectable, rarely troublesome sectors of the Sun Hill area. There might be the occasional burglary, but that would certainly be the work of an outsider. There were no Saturday night punch-ups, no drug peddling, and few complaints about unruly children or domestic flare-ups. You rarely saw more than a few people on the pavements, and

115

then only at the end of a working day or when the women went out shopping.

Today, unusually, there was quite a crowd on one stretch of pavement, with an overflow up the path to the Prices' front door. From one of two cars parked at the kerb a press photographer was lugging his camera and gauging the distance between the pavement and the front of the house. Three women stood back a few yards, unashamedly gawping as Mrs Price opened her front door and began trying to wave the reporters and photographers away.

Burnside stopped close behind the rear car, and got out beside the goggling women.

'Bus stop's along the road, girls.'

They twittered indignantly as he passed, but retreated a few feet.

'Look,' Mrs Price was crying, 'can't you leave us alone? *Please*. We don't want to talk to you, can't you understand, can't you . . .'

Burnside pushed his way through the throng, holding up his warrant card so that she could see it over the bobbing, inquisitive heads. As two pressmen kept trying to elbow their way forward, blocking his route, he said: 'Come on, lads, none of you got kids?'

It had been well meant, a hint rather than a command. The reply was not well meant. 'Yeah, why d'you think I'm here? I've got to feed them, haven't I?'

A photographer took a step to one side, trampling on a compact little flowerbed as he tried for an interesting angle on the distraught young woman in the doorway. Burnside grabbed his wrist and forced the camera downwards. 'Does that thing work when it's been trodden on?'

By the time he released the man, June Ackland had unobtrusively skirted the group and, stepping carefully over the flowerbed and back again, had taken Mrs Price's arm and ushered her back inside. Burnside followed them in and slammed the door shut.

116

'Sorry about that out there. Misery's a big industry. You should have told us you were being hassled.'

'Don't make a lot of difference now, does it?'

The voice came from above. As Burnside looked up, a young man in a green corduroy shirt and old green trousers came slowly downstairs. He had a plump, almost babyish face which you expected to be always smiling, rarely taking anything seriously. Now there was no expression there at all: it was not even a podgy child's face crumpling into misery, but just blank, stunned, uncomprehending.

'Mr Price?'

Burnside held out a hand. Price seemed not even to see it, but walked past him and past a middle-sized dolls' house on a table in the hall, on into the sitting-room. His wife put out a hand as if to catch his arm and draw him close, but he had already brushed past her.

She was slim and, though pale and without makeup, pretty. After the brief outburst during her encounter with the reporters on her doorstep she looked tense and drawn, but not entirely switched off from people and things around her. A button of her light-blue blouse was undone, and her straight brown hair had simply been pulled back into an untidy pony-tail. It was hard to imagine the sheer agony of even getting dressed on a morning like this, pulling the curtains, looking out on to a world that could never, ever, be sane and happy again. But Burnside could see that she was determined to cope. Without her it was impossible to tell whether or not her husband would have forced himself out of bed or made the effort to come downstairs today. Without her it was impossible to imagine how he would be tomorrow, or through the days and weeks after.

Burnside hesitated in the sitting-room doorway and glanced at her, unsure whether or not he should follow Price. She forced a brave smile and waved him in. She and June Ackland came in behind him.

Price was slumped on the sofa, staring at the floor. On the mantelpiece beyond was a colour photograph, probably

117

a school one, of a fresh-faced girl in a brown blazer, with a frank and uninhibited smile enhanced rather than spoilt by a gap in her front teeth. A line of children's paperbacks dominated the small bookcase beside the fireplace. Price looked at nothing but the floor, unwilling to turn his head either way.

'Would you like a coffee or something?' Mrs Price ventured.

Burnside looked out of the window to check on the number of pressmen still loitering and hoping. 'I was wondering if you'd like to come back to Sun Hill, actually. Change of scene. And' – he nodded at the window – 'get the parasites off your back for a while.'

She bent over her husband's bowed head. 'Rob ... Robbie?'

'What?'

It was no more than a whisper.

'Shall we go to the police station?'

'What for?'

Burnside took it gently. 'We have to ask you a few questions. I understood it was okay with both of you. It's just a matter of where and when.'

'Sooner the better now, I think. Not yesterday. I couldn't then.' She slid an arm round her husband's shoulders. 'Maybe a good idea to get out for a bit, Rob, mm?'

'What's the point?' He still did not look up, but was suddenly shouting at the top of his voice into the carpet. An odd, discordant echo rang within a gaudy china souvenir from Lowestoft on top of the television. 'She's dead.'

There was a long silence. At last June Ackland said very quietly: 'Obviously nothing we can say or do is going to alter that, Mr Price.'

'Come on, Robbie.'

After Price's one outburst, the room seemed to grow more and more hushed.

'Honestly,' said Ackland to Mrs Price, 'it doesn't matter right away. We don't want to pressure you.'

118

The girl shook her head. 'We've got to talk about it or we'll both go mad. Robbie . . .?'

Burnside was prepared to give up for now. 'Perhaps tomorrow.'

There was more strength in Mrs Price than her slender body and shy hazel eyes would have suggested. 'No. It's no good putting it off. I've tried to tell him, it's not just us. It could happen to someone else if we don't help. If you don't . . . find him.'

'I don't want to find him,' said Price dully. 'I don't want to see him or know who he is. I don't want to know anything about him.'

'You don't have to, Mr Price.' Ackland was trying to keep her voice on a level with his. 'But your wife's right. He could do it again. We have to stop him. And you can help us by talking about Jennie.'

Mrs Price touched the back of his head. 'You're going to explode otherwise.' Her hand moved down to prise his clenched fist away from the side of his head. He suddenly clutched it and pressed it hard against his cheek. He was starting to shake, sobbing without a sound. Mrs Price slid on to the sofa beside him and let her arm curl round him again.

After a moment she looked up and gave Burnside a little nod.

'We'll wait in the hall,' he said quietly.

When Price had reached up like an automaton to take a reefer jacket from the hall stand, and his wife had shrugged into a russet-coloured raincoat, Ackland opened the front door to let Burnside out first. As the reporters clustered by the gate, Burnside went at them with arms swinging, so that they had to dodge aside to let him through, and the Prices and Ackland close behind him. He flung the back door of the car open and waved the Prices towards it. A couple of men dashed into the road and round the far side, one of them lifting a camera to get a picture of Mrs Price as she slid in close to the nearside rear window. Another man

119

edged round to the front of the car, leaning on the bonnet as if daring Burnside to drive at him.

Burnside went violently into reverse, scattering the group behind and throwing the man at the front off balance, then swung out and forward. Shouts of abuse followed him along the street.

'Wonderful thing, freedom of the press.'

Price sat expressionless in the back seat. His wife kept one hand clenched tightly on her own knee, the other lovingly on his.

Extra chairs had been brought to the incident room. At two of them, two AMIP men were answering a non-stop series of phone calls, not one of which had so far proved of any value whatsoever. People claimed to have seen Jennie Price in a dozen different places where she could not possibly have been alive. There were reports of a group of gipsies staying several nights in the ramshackle factory itself. A meticulous note was made of each.

Mike Dashwood and Tosh Lines were out on their rounds, gathering in the Mouldens and Copes and Bellinghams, the sickly little small-time fumblers who were known for meddling rather than murder. Deadly depressing as the job might be, Ted Roach could not help wondering if he would not rather have been out there on the streets with them or putting the suspects through their paces in the interview room rather than slogging away in the incident room. Out there you stood a chance of getting your hands on things. In here, with nothing solid in front of you, it was like trying to solve a jigsaw in which no two pieces had yet shown any sign of fitting together.

One of the telephone men uttered a courteous acknowledgement, scribbled a note, and slid the paper along the desk towards Roach. He studied it; and began to hope. Not much more than a flicker, but this might be the tip-off they had been waiting for. He turned cheerfully towards Cathy Marshall.

'The winos in Gilfillan Road – none of them mentioned a red car, did they?'

'Only pink lorries carrying puce elephants, and the occasional dog in a red coat. Why, someone reported a sighting?'

'A red car parked near the waste ground.'

Marshall was not over-impressed. 'I expect we'll have the whole rainbow of vehicles by the end of the day. Not to mention seven-wheeled tricycles ridden by six-legged green snakes.'

Roach was not ready to be too optimistic, but five minutes later he brightened a little when another call came through. The first had said merely a red car. The second identified it positively as a Datsun. He could not resist hurrying next door to report the sightings to Meadows.

Meadows did not hesitate to cut him down to size. 'No reg number?'

'Not yet, but I thought you'd want to know.'

Meadows shuffled through some papers which he seemed to find infinitely more fascinating than Roach's news. 'Just mark it in the book. If you get a reg number, then I do want to know. Otherwise stay at your desk. You're the hub of the wheel. Don't let it fall off.'

There was a rap at the door. It was Burnside, escorting Mr and Mrs Price. Meadows immediately forgot Roach's presence, and rose to invite the couple in.

Mrs Price gave Roach a faint, apologetic smile of recognition. 'I'm sorry about yesterday. When you . . . when you came to . . . to tell me. I'm afraid I didn't make it very easy for you.'

There were no words for it. Roach tried to mumble something, touched her arm, and went back to the incident room. This time he would stay put, play it according to the book – the Action Book – and not expect any show of emotion, encouragement, or even of interest from the likes of mealy-mouthed Meadows.

Jimmy Carver, at one of the phone desks, tore off a sheet from a notepad and waved it.

'Ted, we've got a number. The red Datsun. A Mrs Kerrow was bringing her son home from the doctor's about nine-thirty yesterday. The kid remembers the car number because it had his dad's initials: PLK 109W.'

'Have you run a check on it?'

'Give us a chance.'

'Do it, then. Fast.'

After Carver had left the room, Roach grunted dourly at the realization that he had treated him the way Meadows treated people: snap their heads off, treat them with disdain unless they followed all the rules nicely and neatly. Keep down the enthusiasm. Don't be in a hurry to communicate good news until you had found a thousand facts for showing it was definitely not bad news.

Next time he was more cautious, waiting for Meadows to come on his regular tour of inspection in the incident room. By now Carver had done his homework, and it was time to present it to Meadows in the hope of getting a few good marks. The registered owner of the vehicle was a local man: David Charles Kennedy of the Rawminster Road estate. Nothing was known about him. But it was not a savoury area, and there could be some specially unsavoury types there.

'I know Rawminster Road,' said Roach, unable to keep down his excitement in spite of all his resolves. 'It's got some tricky walkways. Easy to do a runner, especially into Crowmont Road. There's an alleyway at either end that links through to the estate. You definitely want TSG backup to plug all the gaps.'

'Thank you, sergeant,' said Meadows mildly. 'Could you circulate the reg number, please. And DC Carver, invite this Mr Kennedy in. TSG 212 for support.'

Carver hurried eagerly out. Things were moving.

'And don't miss the lockups round the back, Jim,' Roach called after him.

In the background they saw Mrs Price, being shown round the premises by June Ackland. Before she could draw closer, Meadows pulled Roach to one side.

'Could you just cool it a bit, Ted? I think professional calm might make a better impression on Mrs Price than your headless chicken act. Oh, and when Mr Kennedy's brought in I'd like to speak to him personally. Understood? But don't worry,' he added placatingly, 'the moment there's any news I'll make sure you're the first to hear.'

Which took Ted Roach's thoughts resentfully back to that whole notion of the good news and the bad news and how Meadows could be relied on to interpret them.

Not that there could ever be what you'd call good news for the Prices. Whatever the outcome, there was no way of striking a happy final balance for them.

Burnside closed the door of the interview room and pulled a chair back for Price to sit on.

'Coffee?'

Price shook his head. Whatever question was asked, that seemed likely to be his stock response.

'The missus won't be long,' said Burnside. 'She was keen to see round the place, see how everything works. Sure you wouldn't rather join her than listen to me?'

Silence.

'Later on,' Burnside persevered, 'we'll need to talk to each of you individually. Not today if you don't feel like it. But sometime. On your own. Normal procedure. That okay?'

Price shrugged.

It was going to be a tricky procedure, putting the man at ease and yet at the same time eliciting essential information.

Burnside said matily: 'I understand you're a motor fitter, Robbie. That right?'

Price summoned up a remote nod.

'Local garage?'

'Worthing's. Tobias Road.'

'Been there long?'

At first it looked as if there was going to be another dead end. Then Price dredged it up indifferently: 'Five years.'

123

'Good firm to work for?' As there were signs of Price slipping back into numbness, Burnside went on: 'So you'd already have gone to work when Jennie left the house yesterday, I suppose?'

Price was looking not at him or the table or the wall of the interview room. He was staring hypnotically into the past, willing it to be wiped out and the present and future changed back into something you could live with. 'I left home at half seven. Jennie was at her window. Upstairs. She waved me off as usual.' The flatness had gone out of his voice. The last few words quivered, and tears were not far away.

A knock at the door broke the shuddering memory. Ackland showed Mrs Price in. As Burnside rose respectfully and turned his chair towards her, she looked past him at her husband.

'They're working so hard for us, Rob. And the phones are ringing all the time, and . . . you know, people who've heard the appeal on the radio and are trying to help. It's really quite amazing.' She turned to Burnside almost in admiration, as if to thank him for the treat of a conducted tour. Then she winced and suddenly, looking back at Price and speaking as blankly as he might have done, she said: 'And then it hits you. They're not looking for Jennie. Jennie's dead. They're not going to bring her back to us. They're just looking for the man who killed her.'

'We'll find him,' said Burnside. 'We will. Believe me.'

He believed it himself, because he had to believe it.

Eleven

The bench in the custody area was beginning to fill up. People who sat on it were rarely a suave, distinguished lot, but today the collection was singularly unprepossessing. Surveying them with distaste, Tosh Lines ticked off names in his notebook. Cope was in Hemel Hempstead and would take time to track down. Tyler, a prime suspect who had been known to resort to impetuous acts of violence, had done just that in a supermarket a week ago and had been in hospital ever since.

Looking at the sullen faces, Mike Dashwood said: 'I suppose I'd better start with Moulden. And what about you having a go at Bellingham?'

Lines followed the angle of his gaze. 'Huh. Only if we go halves.'

Burnside bore down upon them. 'How you doing?'

'How do you think?' said Dashwood dispiritedly. 'Look at 'em. All non-starters, if you ask me.'

'Keep at it. Just wash your hands when you've finished. And keep the brain engaged, Michael.'

'Please, guv, you sound like Ted Roach.'

Turning away, Burnside said over his shoulder: 'Ted's attitude might solve a murder. Yours never will.'

Peeved, Mike Dashwood wheeled the first man into the nearest interview room, settled him in a chair, and went round to sit at the opposite side of the table. There was still a faint smell of new distemper and furniture polish in the room.

Peter Moulden was a skinny youth in his late teens, with unwashed and uncombed hair. His green pullover hung

125

slackly from his scrawny shoulders, shredding into fluff and dangling threads at the elbows. Young as he was, his teeth were already stained and in need of removal. He kept showing them in the vague, disorientated grin of an educationally subnormal drifter.

Dashwood sighed. He had to go through with the routine, but in spite of the DI's injunction he would try to do it without engaging too much of his brain.

'Now, let's be clear about things right from the start, Peter. I'm not arresting you. All we want to do is eliminate you from our enquiries. You do want to be eliminated, don't you?'

'Don't know what it means,' said Moulden, quite genuinely.

'It means' – Dashwood leaned forward – 'that a little girl has been killed. We have a list of people who've offended against little girls. And you're on it.'

This penetrated. Moulden had a spasmodically runny right eye. He wiped it with the back of his hand. 'I wouldn't kill no one.'

'I'm not saying you would. That's why –'

'I ain't even touched no one. Not for ages.'

'But you do hang about outside schools.'

'No, not for ages. I don't do it no more. Honest.'

Dashwood could feel the panic brewing up. He held up both hands in a placatory gesture. 'All right, Peter. Okay.'

But Moulden was growing really agitated. 'I shouldn't be on no list, I don't do nothing, I –'

'All *right*.' Dashwood's own voice rose sharply. 'Just calm down. Tell me where you were yesterday morning. That's all I want to know.'

Moulden began nibbling at a corner of his right thumbnail. Over his pallid knuckles he looked with growing slyness at his interrogator. Then he sniggered. 'In bed.'

'On your own?'

'Yeah.'

'What time did you get up?'

'I didn't.'

'You stayed in bed all day?'

Moulden looked as if he was beginning to enjoy the memory. He nodded, and started on the thumbnail of his left hand.

'Why, were you ill?' When Moulden made a little tittering noise but did not reply, Dashwood prodded him: 'Peter?'

'It's safe in bed,' said Moulden with a vague grin. 'Don't get people looking at you.' He shook his head at Dashwood. 'I shouldn't be on no list no more.'

'Anyone visit you?'

Moulden's grin grew slowly happier, as if he had just remembered something. 'Yes.'

'Who?'

'Simon.'

'Who's Simon?'

Moulden was beaming now. 'My probation officer.'

That would have to be checked out as a matter of course, but Dashwood had a hunch it would prove to be true. There was no joy there.

Next on the list was Bellingham, a complete contrast to the seedy, retarded Peter Moulden. Bellingham was middle-aged and tried to preserve a smart, almost military appearance. His moustache was one of the old-fashioned, bushy but neatly clipped sort favoured by corporals in the regular Army rather than by their officers. He wore a striped tie which might have been in regimental colours, but wasn't. At no time could Bellingham have been accused of getting away with false pretences. He never made any references to his military service, since there had been none; but in his bearing and the occasional modest parrying of a question was something which did not prevent people from thinking of him as an ex-soldier if they chose to.

Tosh Lines, who had hauled him in on three charges in recent years, and helped to have him convicted on one, felt a very special, personal nausea in his presence. Dashwood knew that Tosh would not have trusted himself to carry out an interrogation unaccompanied. The two of them tackled

Bellingham, who settled himself unconcernedly in the interview room and smiled when a cup of coffee was set before him. He took out his own pack of cigarettes and blandly offered them to Lines and Dashwood.

When they refused, Bellingham smiled again and draped one arm over the back of his chair. 'If I had a pound for every time I've been pulled in here I'd be a rich man.'

'You weren't pulled in, Mr Bellingham,' said Lines tightly. 'You agreed to come.'

'Because I've got nothing to hide. I was expecting it, of course. Soon as I heard it on the radio, little girl murdered, I thought "Give them twenty-four hours, they'll be round".'

'You shouldn't be such a scrote,' growled Lines. 'We don't bother decent people.'

'Don't suppose you'll bother the murderer, either.'

'What do you mean by that?' Dashwood demanded.

Bellingham tapped cigarette ash a fraction of an inch away from the ashtray and shook his head in mocking apology. 'Two of you talking to *me*? Doesn't exactly suggest hard evidence elsewhere, does it?'

Lines said: 'Where were you yesterday morning from eight-forty-five onwards?'

'Well . . .' Bellingham deliberately took his time over it. 'I'd had a bit of a booze-up the night before.' Archly he anticipated their question: 'Adults only, naturally. So I never got up till gone nine. Then I went to the bottle bank, because I'm very eco-conscious. And then to the video shop, because they charge an arm and a leg if you keep the things for two days.'

'Tasty, were they – the videos?' suggested Dashwood.

Bellingham pursed his lips regretfully. 'Very tame, actually. I wouldn't recommend them for your next social. Strictly over the counter.'

'Not your usual party fare, then? Not the stuff for corrupting minors?'

Bellingham summoned up a reproachful stare. 'I thought we were into murder today, not child abuse.'

128

'What video shop?' snapped Lines.

'Star Tape. Elidor Parade.'

'Time?'

'At the shop? About ten-thirty. Carla was serving. She'll remember. And of course,' said Bellingham airily, 'I left the wheelbarrow outside.'

'Wheelbarrow?'

'How else did I get this kid over to Gilfillan Road? I don't drive. You know that – since it was you who fixed that up for me.'

Lines turned away, rigid with the need for self-control. 'Turn him out, Mike. Before I stick *him* in a wheelbarrow.'

As Dashwood came back past the incident room after escorting the cockily strutting Bellingham out, he heard Ted Roach's characteristic splutter and Bob Cryer's equally characteristic crisp, I've-seen-it-all answer.

'Well, of course he'd want to interview Kennedy personally, wouldn't he? If the man coughs, Meadows gets the glory. You'll do the same when you're a superintendent.'

'Huh. When.'

'And why not, anyway? It's him who carries the can if we don't make an arrest.'

'I'm not impressed. It shows a small mind.'

'What do you expect, Hercules Poirot? Meadows works to a formula, Ted. We all do, if we're honest. And sometimes it works. Sometimes it doesn't. Right, Cathy?'

Cathy Marshall recited her gospel: 'Screen out, sift, and collate.'

'Yeah, well, I just hope Kennedy's our man,' said Roach. 'And to hell with glory.'

Dashwood was only too ready to echo those sentiments. They had had no joy so far. They could only hope that Jimmy Carver and his sidekick would bring in a bonus: the owner of that unexplained parked car, plus good news.

DC Carver and the AMIP man assigned to him crossed the littered, hard-trodden grass of the council estate and climbed the stairs to a second-floor balcony. The second DC was silent, as he had been for most of the way here. Carver found his presence disturbing. For all he knew, there was some secretive assessment of his own capabilities being carried out along with the murder investigation: something about Detective Superintendent Meadows' whole attitude suggested this was not impossible. If anything went wrong with this inquiry, all the blame was liable to be shifted on to Sun Hill personnel.

Jimmy Carver counted along the front doors to make sure he found the right one. It was not a simple matter of looking for the number. The glass panels of several doors had been smashed in, and sheets of chipboard hammered across the whole framework. It seemed reasonable to assume, though, that the unidentified Number 7 was the one lying between Number 6 and Number 8. There was no spacing out in even or uneven sequences here: nobody was likely to build opposite.

If there had been a knocker or a bellpush, both had disappeared. He banged hard on the wooden panel. After a pause he banged again. At last the door was opened, though still on a chain, by a light-coloured West Indian woman in her twenties. Her tightly frizzed hair was dyed bright orange, clashing violently with her red and black striped sweater. Her eyes were at once suspicious and defensive.

'Morning.' Carver showed his warrant card. 'DC Carver, Sun Hill Police. We're looking for Mr Kennedy.'

'What for?'

'Are you Mrs Kennedy, love?'

The woman shook her head, setting her long, dangling earrings a-chatter.

'But David Kennedy does live here?' Carver persevered.

'If you say so.'

'Is he in?'

'No.'

'Maybe we could come in?'

'No.'

Carver advanced his right foot in case she tried to shut
130

the door on him. 'Well, do you know where Mr Kennedy is? It's very important that we speak to him.'

She stayed just as sullen, poised as if to justify his belief that she was likely to close the door. Then she looked at the faces of the two officers, disliked what she saw, but obviously decided to go grudgingly along with them.

'He's fixing the car.'

'Where? Here on the estate?'

'No.'

There was a call from the direction of the vehicle parking and turning space below. Jimmy Carver moved to the balcony railing and looked down. A TSG officer was offering him a 'no-result' wave. While he had been engaged up aloft, their tour had produced no trace of the red Datsun on the estate itself.

Carver leaned over and shouted: 'What about the lockups? No joy there?'

The man shook his head.

Behind Carver the woman said: 'Didn't I just tell you, he's not here.' She was beginning to look alarmed at the realization that while two policemen were on the balcony outside her door, others had been secretly sniffing around below.

'So you did. But you didn't get round to saying where he actually is.'

'Any reason why I should?'

'Save us a lot of time. Unless, of course, you've got some reason for not letting on.'

'His brother's. Lunnis Road.'

'Number?'

It had to be dragged out of her. 'Fourteen.'

'You wouldn't mess us about, would you, love?'

But this time she had decided that she had had enough, and it was time to close the door. Maybe she wished she had stayed mum at the back of the flat and never even opened it in the first place.

So they would have to give Lunnis Road a spin. On the way, Carver contacted the Sun Hill incident room, to be greeted by Ted Roach's increasingly irate bark. He reported his destination, and was roughly advised to keep the TSG with him: Lunnis Road did not indulge in anything so civilized as Neighbourhood Watch.

It was certainly not one of the more salubrious streets on the manor. The terraces of houses could well have been trim and unpretentious in the late nineteenth century, the domain of quiet middle-class clerks and slightly superior shop assistants. Today they had no pretensions whatsoever and had long since ceased to be trim. It was surprising that they had not long ago been replaced by more high-rise blocks of flats. But terraces or flats, they would always be infected by a dusty despair, and subjected to a constant racket from a railway viaduct at the end.

Nevertheless there was one pretty sight to reward Jimmy Carver's eyes. Standing by the kerb with its bonnet up was a red Datsun; and its registration number was PLK 109W. A pair of long legs in blue overalls sprawled languidly out from underneath.

Carver treated himself to a slow stroll across the street and, after a moment of contemplation, tapped his right shoe against the protruding left foot.

A tall young West Indian rolled himself out on an inspection trolley and looked up quizzically.

'Mr David Kennedy?' When the young man nodded, Carver produced his warrant card. 'We're police officers, sir. I wonder if we could ask you a few questions?'

Kennedy heaved himself up to his feet, wiping his hands down the sides of his overall. He looked puzzled rather than worried as he waved them towards the open front door of the house overlooking the parked car. 'My brother's place,' he explained as they went in and turned right into an untidy room with a pile of trucking magazines spilling over in one corner, and a portable radio sitting in the middle of the floor. A telephone was fastened to the wall immediately inside the door.

Carver noticed his AMIP shadow sizing up the room as

132

if to memorize it against the time when every detail would have to be recorded and, hopefully, used in court.

Kennedy sustained his easy going lack of concern as Carver prudently asked innocuous questions about the Datsun, where it was usually kept, and where it had been over the last couple of days. Yes, it was true that it had been in Gilfillan Road yesterday morning. And yes, it was quite close to that derelict site near the old factory. It just happened that way. Then, before any further questions could be asked, the import of what was being said dawned on Kennedy. The name of Gilfillan Road jelled with what he had heard on the radio. It seemed never to have occurred to him to connect the two until now. First he looked incredulous; and it was several minutes before a sultry anger began to glow in his eyes.

'Just a minute, you're not accusing me of –'

'We're accusing nobody of anything, sir,' said Carver. 'But we do need to know why your car was there at that particular time yesterday . . . and what you yourself were doing there.'

'I wasn't there. Not yesterday morning.'

'Then what was the car doing there?' asked Carver patiently.

His patience earned him a poor reward. The car had undoubtedly been in Gilfillan Road at the time reported. Kennedy did not deny that. The trouble was that it had also been there the previous night and most of the day before that. 'Broken down,' said Kennedy grumpily. He produced the receipt for a new battery, dated the previous day. He also, half indignant but by now understanding the need to confirm his innocence, gave Carver the phone number of the recovery firm from which he had tried to get a tow. Carver phoned them, to find that they remembered Mr Kennedy well enough: he had been unable to pay cash, and not for the first time, so they would not play ball.

There was now another phone call Jimmy Carver had to make. He was not looking forward to the outcome. Praise and jubilation were not on the agenda. There was every reason to

133

suppose that neither Ted Roach nor the overbearing Meadows would be filled with rapture.

Frank Burnside was not used to keeping his voice muted to a sympathetic level for long periods at a time. But with Mr and Mrs Price sitting across the table from him, he was at a loss how else to proceed. Even the quietest of questions sounded like an insult or a heartless provocation of more grief from the two of them. He knew, too, that June Ackland was listening sadly and critically to every word. He would be glad to get out of this room, out of this whole foul business; and knew there was only one way he could hope to get out. He had to go on and on asking the questions, asking doggedly away, until the answers could be added up to a satisfactory total.

Quietly he proceeded. 'Jennie always walked to school on her own, did she?'

'Most days, yes.' Mrs Price was very calm, but the strain was bringing little hairline fractures into her voice. 'I always used to take her, but this year she wanted to start going on her own. Growing up, you know.' She could not restrain an instinctive smile, half affectionate, half proud. 'It's only a six- or seven-minute walk.'

She built up a picture of Jennie's movements as if they were still real and everyday, had happened this very morning and would happen again tomorrow and right through the school term. Growing up . . . not that she ever would, now.

The girl had always gone the same way to school, not meeting with any friends, except that on Fridays – pocket money day – she had gone via the corner shop in Jacey Grove. Her regular Friday treat was to buy a packet of crisps for break time. But so far as Mrs Price knew, she had not gone along Jacey Grove on the day of her disappearance.

'And was she happy,' Burnside ventured, 'when she left home?'

'Jennie's always happy.' Then Mrs Price heard the resonance of her own words inside her head, and said: 'She was always happy.'

134

At last it had become too much. She broke down, sobbing. Her husband got up and put his arm round her, just as she had done to him earlier. 'Come on, we're going home.'

'No.' She fought her way back through the tears. 'It's got to be done, Rob.'

'Not today it hasn't.'

Mrs Price's determination was enough to make June Ackland weep silently to herself, not letting any of the rest of them see it. Burnside felt it, out of some corner of his always professional awareness; and took care not to look round. He waited until Price, on his feet, slowly let himself be lulled into sitting down again.

'Jennie never mentioned seeing anything odd on her way to or from school, did she? Never spoken to by a stranger? You know, an adult – someone with a dog, maybe?'

'She liked dogs,' said Mrs Price reflectively.

Hadn't there been something about the boy Graeme Butler liking dogs, too? But that shattered, downcast school caretaker had been eliminated from their enquiry. Only Burnside himself had not been present at the questioning. He wondered how reliable the results had been. How many steps would they have to retrace to get back near the time and scene of the killings?

'Did she know many adults – felt at ease with them?'

'Well, family of course. My sister and her husband. Rob's got two brothers. And his dad.'

'What about friends of the family?' Burnside could not assess what sort of quicksand he might be walking into. 'Acquaintances? Anyone who maybe knew Jennie more than they knew Robbie and yourself?'

Rob Price stirred after a long reverie. 'What are you asking us to do – point a finger at somebody we know?'

'No,' said Burnside unconvincingly.

Price was wider awake than he would have thought. 'Sounds like it.'

'Just routine questions, I assure you. But I do have to ask them to get everything out of the –'

'Routine? Like asking me to explain my movements yesterday morning?' Price was abruptly on his feet, slamming his fist rhythmically down, up and down on the table. 'You've got half the Met here, mate, or that's the way it looks. Is this the best you can do? Look ... I was her father. She was all we had. All we ever wanted. And now she's gone. And you ... you never solved that little boy's murder, and you won't solve this one either. Because you're useless, the whole damn lot of you. So just shut up and leave us alone.'

His wife was reaching for him, tugging him down and stroking his arm. There was no way of getting through to him, and for once in his life Burnside felt it would be sinful to attempt it. He could not possibly know what Rob Price was going through right now, but he tried to imagine it; and then gave up trying to imagine it. There were things you couldn't touch, couldn't bear to touch.

He left it for several minutes until Price raised his head, saying nothing but looking straight at him as though steeling himself for the inquisition to continue.

Burnside said: 'Is there anyone you two could stay with for a few days? Relatives or friends? Now they've got your home address, the press aren't going to let go, even with a copper on the door.'

'My sister's offered,' said Mrs Price remotely.

'Take her up on it. Right now, if you can face it.'

Mrs Price nodded. She was the one who clearly had to make the decisions.

He was glad for the tap on the door that called him away for a few minutes, leaving them to talk to each other and sort it out; or simply sit there together, silent, because there was nothing they dared to talk about. His relief was soon soured. The call was to inform him that the Datsun driver could be eliminated from the enquiries. The car had simply broken down, there was plenty of evidence to confirm that, and nothing to suggest that Kennedy was ever likely to have been involved in child murder. Nothing pointed that way.

Roughing up his girlfriend every now and then, maybe; attacking kids, no.

Glumly Burnside made his way to the incident room.

Meadows greeted him in similar mood. 'You've heard about Kennedy?'

'Yes, sir.'

'What about the Prices?'

'They've had enough for one day. I thought you'd like to see them before we shift them. Mrs Price has got a sister, good for them to stay there, keep the vultures circling somewhere else.'

Meadows disregarded this last opinion, anxious for another. 'And what do you reckon?'

Burnside stalled. 'We've only had a preliminary chat. I haven't had either of them on their own for long.'

'All the same,' Meadows insisted, 'what do you reckon?'

'Price?' Burnside gave him a long, hard stare. 'No way, sir.'

'Pity.'

Meadows headed out. Watching him go, Roach said bitterly: 'Well, it would have been helpful, I suppose, if the parents had done it.'

Burnside could have slapped him down. Or preferably Meadows. He was in a mood to do so.

The process of screening out, sifting, and collating had to go on its weary way. They had gone through the possibilities of the parents, a collection of perverts, and the owner of a clapped-out car, and so far had got nowhere. They had started with two dog hairs and a fingerprint, and that was exactly what they had still got.

'It's only Day One, Ted,' Mike Dashwood said hearteningly.

'Sure. And by Day Three everyone'll start losing interest, and gradually there'll be talk of stretched resources and priorities and cash allocations. Some accountant up there in the clouds will send down a balance sheet telling us at exactly what level of expenditure to cut off. And I don't want that. I don't want another kid murdered because we've just been going through the motions, all according to the book . . . only no one can be bothered to give this book a happy ending.'

'So what ending do you have in mind?' asked Dashwood. 'How do you actually catch a child killer?'

'I don't bloody well know.' Angry with himself and the world in general, Roach burst out: 'I don't know any more than Meadows.' He slammed the Action Book shut. 'I just care a bit more, maybe.'

'Wearing your heart on your sleeve never solved a crime yet.'

Before Roach could blast back a retort, the phone rang. He picked it up, and his nose wrinkled in displeasure. The voice of Meadows was the last thing he wanted to hear at this stage of the proceedings. But obediently he said: 'Yes, sir. Right with you.' He waved Dashwood towards his chair. 'Hold the fort.'

He went along to Meadows' office, to find the superintendent chatting with a dark-suited middle-aged man who momentarily avoided looking at Roach on his arrival.

'Ted.' Meadows sounded unusually, unconvincingly affable. 'Want you to meet DS Paul Gavin. He'll be taking over the Action Book from tomorrow.'

'Sir?'

'I did tell you that you were just filling in, didn't I?'

'No, sir, you didn't.'

Roach knew that Meadows knew damn well he had neither said nor implied any such thing.

'Anyway,' Meadows went blandly on, 'fortunately Paul has been made available to me, and we know each other's methods, so you'll be able to get back on the streets where you feel more at home.' When there was no reply, Meadows nodded a dismissal. 'I'll send him through in a minute for an update.'

Ted Roach stood outside the office door for a moment,

his stomach curling in on itself. Or maybe it was his lungs, deciding to give up the effort of breathing in and out. He saw PC Steve Loxton heading towards him, and pulled himself together as Loxton went past. Then he walked off towards the incident room and, after one glance through the glass panel, past it. Dashwood had been on the phone in there, but now came hurrying out.

'Bad news on the fingerprint. The one on the plastic sack. It's not known.'

'Too bad,' said Ted Roach dully. 'You'd better tell Meadows, not me.'

Twelve

Ted Roach was back with a vengeance on the streets where, Meadows had sneered, he would feel more at home. Maybe it was true. Maybe this was, after all, the only sort of atmosphere in which he could breathe properly. In front of him this Thursday morning there certainly lay the sort of challenge he had always been eager to accept, getting his teeth into obvious, meaty facts and worrying them like a dog stripping a bone to its clean, glistening core.

A large truck stood by the slimy kerb of a back street half a mile from Sun Hill. Both sides of the street were lined with the rear walls of shops, and the slime on the pavement came from rubbish which was supposed to have been thrown into wheelie-bins but had all too often missed. You could tell by the colours and constituents of the débris which was the back door of the Chinese takeaway and which the door of the DIY centre. The back doors of the truck itself were wide open, but nothing had been shed from it: or, rather, what had been shed would have been spotless, and had been spirited away without leaving a mark. Ten grand's worth of CD players had gone missing, along with six grand's worth of pocket tape recorders and three grand's worth of food mixers, all off-loaded in broad daylight while nobody, apparently, saw a thing. Perhaps the locals had not wanted to get mixed up in food mixers. Or perhaps a good handful of them had been too thoroughly mixed up in the whole affair.

Ted Roach and Mike Dashwood drove the truck driver back to Sun Hill and settled down to make a statement. The man, Kenning, was in his middle forties, dressed in a green boiler suit and looking very straightforward and confident.

He calmly confirmed that he had locked up the wagon and gone into the café for breakfast. He always had a bite to eat around that time. Then when he came out, the vehicle was gone. He had reported it to the police at once, and, as they knew, had hurried along to identify the vehicle once they had found it. He could remember exactly what he had had on board, and the delivery sheets in the cab confirmed this.

Roach found Kenning's cool confidence a bit fishy. It did not sit well on a man who had just lost a valuable cargo of goods and ought to have been fretting about what his employer would say, and fretting about the way he himself had been made to look a fool. Yet he seemed in calm possession of himself, and unworried about the outcome of this or any other interview.

Roach made an excuse to slip from the room and have a quick word with DI Burnside. His impression was that Kenning was sharper than he made himself out to be, and was so smooth and well-rehearsed that he must have played this kind of game before. But they had nothing on which to hold him; and once he was out, you could be sure that the stuff would disappear for good, if it had not already been distributed.

'Right.' Burnside made a swift decision. 'Wind him right up, bung him back out on the street, give him half an hour to get home, then find a reason to pull him back in here.'

'Might do the trick. Could always bring him back via the scenic route, give him some verbal . . .'

'Tut, tut, tut.' Burnside wagged his head. 'Interrogating a suspect in the rear of a police car is against procedure, old son. Mind you' – he twisted his little finger in his ear as he strolled away – 'my hearing really has got bad of late. Didn't hear a word you just said.'

Chief Superintendent Brownlow said: 'It seems to me that there's been too much cutting corners in this station. Uniform and CID, it's getting worrying. Nothing too dangerous as yet, but I'd appreciate your tidying up some procedures before we find ourselves in an embarrassing situation.'

It was his regular conference with Chief Inspector Conway and Inspector Monroe. The other two were accustomed to the chief super coming up with some earnest generalization at the beginning of each meeting. He somehow felt that it would keep them on their toes. Once it was out of the way, they could get down to routine business.

For once, however, Monroe was quick to agree. He had brought with him three sheets of lined paper covered with neat handwriting, and was about to explain them when Brownlow made it plain he had not yet finished.

'As I mentioned at our last meeting, we are well overdue for a visit from the Forces Inspectorate team. I now have confirmation that we shall have a full-scale inspection two months from now, under Commander Roy Godfrey. His front runners will be Chief Superintendent Braun and Chief Inspector Willis. They are due here next week for a pre-inspection tour. Next week,' Brownlow emphasized. 'You've had fair warning. I trust you'll ensure that the I's are dotted and the T's crossed in all areas of procedure.'

So that was what he had been leading up to. Conway relaxed. 'I think you'll find we're watertight, sir. A few minor details, yes, I can see your point; but I for one have every confidence that Commander Godfrey and his team will leave with smiles on their faces.'

'I'm pleased to hear it, Derek.' Brownlow looked at Monroe. 'Andrew?'

'I'm sorry, sir, I don't share Mr Conway's confidence.'

The chief inspector stared from one to the other, his mouth falling open.

'I'm sorry to hear that, Andrew,' said Brownlow, ominously quiet.

Monroe separated two sheets of his handwritten notes and handed one to each of them.

'When you marked our cards at the last meeting, sir, about

a possible visit from the Inspectorate, I thought I would pre-empt –'

'What the blazes is this?' Conway was furious.

'I think I did mention it to you, sir.' But Monroe was concentrating on Brownlow. 'It's a report I have compiled over the last week, highlighting areas where in my opinion we are not operating according to the accepted ground rules.'

'And you've put it all down on paper?' Conway stared rancorously at the tidy lines of handwriting before him.

'There are only three copies, all of which are in this room.'

'Well, at least that's something to be thankful for.'

Brownlow said: 'Obviously we ought to read and consider this, Derek, before continuing the meeting, since it may well be relevant to our further discussion.'

'Sir,' said Conway, still staring with repugnance at his sheet of paper.

'Let's say we resume in half an hour, right?'

Conway and Monroe left. Conway, not trusting himself to make any comment, swung abruptly away down the corridor and went back to his office. He had just finished reading the report when Brownlow put his head round the door.

'Food for thought, eh, Derek?'

'And quite a score on brownie points, sir.'

Brownlow eased himself into the office. 'Derek, it's never a question of point scoring with Andrew. He's not that kind of animal.'

'It's a matter of professional courtesy, sir. I'd have liked to have the chance to read and discuss his findings before –'

'All right, yes. To some extent I appreciate your attitude. But with my warning you of the impending inspection, I suppose Andrew felt he must get things down in the right order in a hurry. And whatever you may think, his report does highlight one or two procedural problems within this station.'

'With all due respect, sir, there are always bound to be one or two minor problems regarding procedure. Quite apart

143

from current hangovers from the rebuilding and that Barton Street spell, we're constantly being subjected to rule and procedural changes on almost a daily basis.'

'You're not telling me anything I don't already know, Derek. The plain fact of the matter is that Andrew's report also points out very clearly that certain individuals within this station are prone to cut corners on a regular basis. I've already commented on that myself. I don't have to tell you how easy it is for that sort of thing to become habitual, and very soon taken as a matter of normal procedure.'

Conway accepted defeat. 'I'll study the report in more detail, sir, and come back to you.' But, turning the paper over as if it were contaminating his fingertips, he could not resist one final thrust. 'All the same, if it comes to cutting corners and ignoring procedures, there ought to be some mention of Burnside's little mob.'

'CID don't come within Andrew's brief. You know that. In any case,' Brownlow smiled in anticipation, 'I fancy that when Gordon Wray settles in with us he'll put a stop to a lot of Frank Burnside's little manoeuvres.'

Roach and Dashwood led Kenning across the parking space of the rundown block of flats from which they had just extracted him. He looked a lot less confident than before, but made up for it by being forcefully indignant.

'Why the hell aren't you out looking for the geezers who nicked my load, not coming round to waste my time?'

'You know how it is, sir,' said Roach gravely. 'We have to do everything according to the book. You'd be the first to complain if we messed things up because of some silly irregularity.'

'You blokes are on a wind-up.'

Dashwood opened the passenger door of the car.

'Very sorry about this, Mr Kenning,' Roach continued. 'Just that within ten minutes of you leaving the station we realized you hadn't signed your statement.' He smiled apologetically. 'Entirely our mistake.'

'I'll sign it now, right here.'

'Sorry, it has to be done down the station, Mr Kenning.'

'Yeah, I figured you'd say that.'

Muttering words which rarely exceeded four letters, Kenning climbed into the back seat. Roach slid in beside him, while Mike Dashwood settled into the driver's seat. They were both smiling in what might have been taken as a friendly way. Kenning did not take it that way, but stared sullenly ahead.

'Now, my old pal,' said Roach comfortably, 'we're going to do you a favour.'

'That so? Tell me about it.'

'Look, Mr Kenning,' said Dashwood over his shoulder, 'we're not a pair of old mugs. We know the SP.'

'You know sweet FA, pal.' Kenning looked contemptuously out of the window, then tensed. 'Oi, this isn't the way to the nick.'

'Short cut, Mr Kenning. Nothing to worry about.'

'Yeah, you must think I'm the old mug an' all, then. But you'll find I'm not.'

He had regained his old complacency. There was something almost gloating in his tone that gave Ted Roach a twinge of unease.

Burnside greeted them brightly as they escorted Kenning towards an interview room.

'Well, well! Back so soon, old son?'

'Get stuffed.'

'You're the one that's going to get stuffed, old son, well and truly.' Burnside turned to Roach. 'A quiet word in your shell-like.'

Dashwood kept Kenning on the move as Roach reported in an undertone. 'He didn't fall for it, guv. He knows the score.'

'Too right he does. Must have been on the phone the moment he got back home, even before you went for him. Must have expected it. His brief arrived here five minutes ago. Guessing well ahead, wouldn't you say?'

'Oh, terrific.'

'Innocent men aren't that well organized,' said Burnside. 'Now we know, it'll be no sweat. Just run it by the book from here on in. It's only a matter of time and we'll have him bang to rights.'

Ted Roach, feeling a lot less sure of that, went on his way to join Dashwood and Kenning in the interview room. Kenning had already established himself in the same lounging, unruffled attitude he had preserved throughout the first interrogation. It had been routine then, he implied, and it was going to stay routine. No sweat, Burnside had said. No sweat at all, by the look of it, so far as Kenning was concerned.

Roach plunged in. 'Let's stop mucking about, Mr Kenning. We know you're on the firm, and it's only a matter of time.'

'If you're a sensible boy,' Dashwood contributed, 'we'll put in a good word for you and things will go easy on you from here on in.'

Kenning smirked, but before he could say whatever he had in mind the door opened and Inspector Monroe came in.

'Look, that man out there's been waiting at least ten minutes. When are you going to –'

'You the guvnor?' Kenning stood up, producing a miniature tape recorder from his inside pocket and laying it on the table. 'Just the man I want to see.' He reached out to click on the recorder. 'You might be interested in this. They're fitting me up.' He wound the machine back, then pressed the play button.

'We're going to do you a favour.' It was unmistakably Roach's voice.

'That so? Tell me about it.'

'Look, Mr Kenning' – identifiably Dashwood – 'we're not a pair of old mugs. We know the SP.'

Kenning switched off and grinned smugly at Roach and Dashwood. 'And I told you I wasn't a mug either, remember?' He swung towards Monroe. 'That was recorded in the back of their motor. Now, where's my brief?'

Roach and Dashwood bent before the blistering accusation in Inspector Monroe's gaze.

PC Dave Quinnan had been ambling his usual way between the stalls of the street market, enjoying himself simply because he was wearing a police uniform and in a position to chat people up or round them up, whatever was in vogue at any given moment. One of the traders, bobbing out from the side of his secondhand clothes stall, tried to ingratiate himself by waving a scarlet jumper in front of Quinnan's tunic and raising a matey eyebrow.

'What size are you?'

'Sorry Reg, that's classified info.'

Reg looked mystified, not sure whether or not to take this seriously. Dolly, from the next stall, chipped in. 'Don't ask him the time of day neither, Reg. You want to know the time of day, don't ask a policeman. Not any more. That's classified information and all.'

Quinnan shook his head in mock reproach. He felt at home in the middle of this joky chit-chat; knew the language and revelled in it.

After school in south London he had trained as an electrician, worked as a jobbing spark, and then moved up to Aberdeen when there was money on the rigs. The youngest of five children, with a father who had been injured in an industrial accident and been given precious little in compensation, he had always had an idealistic eye on a fat wage packet. When the oil bubble burst, he returned south and joined the Met, serving his probationary years at Bow Street. Money was the chief reason for joining the Force, but he had to admit he enjoyed the exercise of authority, and was not above pushing that a little when the going got rough. He was getting paid for punishing wrongdoers, wasn't he? If he had wanted to help people, he would have joined the Samaritans. But he hadn't.

'Hey,' Dolly was ranting on, 'when are you lot going to do something about them gippos under the flyover?'

'Just as soon as the council sort themselves out, we'll move them.' Quinnan had said it a dozen times before.

'The day that bunch of wallies sort themselves out, that'll be the day they open a Conservative Club in Red Square.'

Her neighbour edged over to nudge her in the ribs. 'Here, you never know, Dolly. With all this perrystrikin' and glasfingy going on . . .'

Quinnan, in no hurry to leave the convivial surroundings, glanced across the street at the pub which had opened some twenty minutes ago. There was not much trade at this hour of the morning, but before noon several stallholders would find excuses to saunter in, keeping an eye on their stalls through the plain glass above the ornate Victorian gilded lettering and curlicues. He might drop in himself, in a sociable sort of way, to check that everything was going smoothly and legally and the landlord had no formal complaints. You had to keep in with the regulars: there was no telling when their chat might come in handy.

A man in a bulging raincoat was leaving the pub. He must have got there early, and decided to leave early. Quinnan, only mildly curious at first, found himself wondering what the bulky object might be under the departing customer's coat. He had a feeling he had seen that unprepossessing type before, and not in especially commendable circumstances.

The man quickened his pace. Quinnan, leaving Reg and Dolly in mid-conversation, began to trot after him.

A side street from the market led to a stretch of corrugated fencing with some gaps in it, through which were visible some hummocks of waste land. Quinnan saw the end of a light brown raincoat twitching through one of the gaps, and headed for the same opening.

Beyond, there was nobody in sight. The area might have been a designated junkyard, but it was doubtful if any authority had bothered with a designation. Householders all around the space had decided to use it as their own

148

private rubbish tip. Quinnan picked his way over sacks, cans, and crumpled boxes. After a few minutes wandering aimlessly in circles, he stopped and listened.

The thunder of traffic from the flyover made it difficult to pick out lesser sounds. But there was something that he was sure meant breaking glass. He edged cautiously off to his right and peered down into the basement area of a house which did not look as if it had sheltered any home-loving inhabitants for a long time.

His prey was down there, carefully shoving fragments of glass to one side and picking out coins from the jagged mess. He shovelled them into his pocket and kicked the neck of a large bottle out of the way. When he straightened up and looked up, his greedy face sagged into disbelief and utter despair.

'Oh, no.'

'Oh, yes,' said Quinnan benevolently. 'Now come on up out of there, sunshine.'

It gave him a feeling of warm accomplishment to march the miserable little creep back to Sun Hill, sending out a radio message on his way, and deliver him to Sergeant Peters at the charge desk.

The sergeant stared at the new arrival. 'Good God, it's Peter the Ponce. Haven't seen you for ages. Not that I'm complaining.'

Quinnan said: 'Peters the . . .?'

'In the singular, if you don't mind.' Alec Peters turned his attention to the pile of coins tipped on to his desk. 'The children's Christmas party bottle! That's it, isn't it? The *Green Man* start that early every year. For kids. And you . . . you sticky-fingered little git . . .'

Quinnan said: 'I've contacted the governor of the pub, sarge. He'll pop in after the lunchtime rush.'

'Good.' Peters counted out the coins punctiliously, finishing with a total of twenty-eight pounds eighty-seven pence, an Irish shilling, and two pesetas. He wrote it down and pushed the form towards the cringing little man. 'Sign there. And there's a nice cold cell all ready and waiting for you, Peter.'

'I didn't nick the bottle, sarge. I found it where he nicked me, honest – just lying there it was, and –'

'Just lying? Like you. And the moon is made of cheese and stuffed with bull's droppings.' He stooped and jangled his ring of cell keys. 'Shall I show you to your room, sir?'

'Oh don't bang me up, sarge.'

Peters nodded his wish that he should be promptly relieved of his unwelcome burden. Quinnan hastened to step alongside his capture. 'Move it, sunshine.' But Peter the Ponce seemed in no mood to move. He was still whining against fate, but it had become a more piercing, insistent whine.

'I got information. I want to see someone from CID.' As they wearily shook their heads he began to screech it out. 'Straight up, I got some info, be worth your while . . .'

'Don't muck me about,' said Peters.

'Someone from CID! I'm not kidding.'

'And I'm not listening.'

'Mr Burnside, I want to see Mr Burnside.'

Peters and Quinnan exchanged glances. It might be just a desperate attempt to scrounge a way out of the mess. On the other hand, someone like this might be just the sort of little creep who might be expected to have some smelly little morsel of foul information that the devious DI would appreciate.

Dave Quinnan went to fetch Burnside.

As Peters pulled back the Judas flap in the cell door, Burnside looked in and groaned.

'Peter the Ponce?' He scornfully closed the flap. 'A two-bit ponce. A lowlife who should have been put down at birth for the good of mankind.'

'I'll second that,' said Peters.

'But,' said Quinnan, 'he does claim to have information, sir.'

Burnside chewed for a thoughtful moment on his lower lip. On impulse he opened the flap again and gazed in. He waited for Peter the Ponce to raise his head, and grated: 'You say you wanted something?'

He did not invite Quinnan into the subsequent brief session in the interview room. But when he emerged, it was clear that he had done some kind of deal and was optimistic about results. He wanted the man set free. Overruling Peters' formal protests, he promised to take full responsibility for any problems later. Not that there would be any problems: he intended to come back with the goods.

Sergeant Peters and Dave Quinnan watched dubiously as Burnside led Peter the Ponce to the door opening on to the yard, patting him on the back – warningly rather than affectionately.

'You just remember, if you're wetting up my leg I'll come looking for you.'

'It's kosher, Mr Burnside, straight up. I wouldn't con you.'

'It would be very unwise, old son. I'd have you put away for two score and ten, and I'd make sure you went down as a nonce job. Just so you could be sure of getting the right treatment from the other inmates. You get me?'

'Yes, Mr Burnside.'

'Right. Now get.'

They watched him go. Burnside wore an expression the other two recognized, having seen it often enough in varying circumstances: admiration of his own brilliance and know-how, all meriting acknowledgement and a round of applause in the very near future.

At the front desk, a smartly dressed man with a briefcase under his arm paced to and fro. WPC Datta had courteously suggested that he should sit down while waiting for an answer to the message she had passed through to the officers interviewing his client, Mr Kenning. She was sure they wouldn't be long. But the solicitor had no intention of sitting down. His steady trudge from end to end of the limited space declared that every minute which passed would be an

151

additional black mark on his assessment of police behaviour in the present persecution of his entirely innocent client.

A less aggressive man arrived at the desk and answered Norika Datta's polite query with a friendly smile.

'Joe Timson. I'm the guvnor down at the *Green Man*, Farquhar Street. One of your blokes phoned earlier and asked me to call in.'

'Could you give me a little more detail and the name of the officer, sir?'

'Don't know his name, but he says he collared the toe-rag who nicked the cash bottle off my bar this morning.'

'Ah. I think we've let him out, actually.'

'Let him out?'

'Hold on, I'll make enquiries. Won't keep you long.'

Norika Datta's warm voice soothed many an awkward customer at the desk. It had failed to soothe the waiting solicitor, and now seemed to be having little effect on Mr Timson. He was about to protest when Sergeant Peters, summoned by Datta, came hurriedly through and took him aside.

Lumbered with the aftermath of Frank Burnside's decision, Alec Peters was thinking on his feet. 'What it amounts to, Mr Timson, is that we have managed to retrieve the cash. I know you'll be pleased about that.'

'Yes, but –'

'We've been waiting,' said Peters accommodatingly, 'to see what you want to do about it.'

'Hold on a minute. Are you trying to tell me that you haven't nicked the toe-rag that stole that bottle?'

'Oh yes, we've arrested him, but . . . er . . . it's not quite that simple, Mr Timson.'

'What d'you mean, it's not that simple? You either collared him or you didn't. When your bloke phoned me this morning, he was dead keen for me to come down and press charges. I'm here and I want to do just that. And I'll tell you what – I'm not moving from here until I do.'

Peters closed his eyes in silent prayer. When he opened them, Inspector Monroe was in the room, his brow dark with the effects of whatever storm had blown up while he was in the adjoining room with Roach and Dashwood.

'Any problems, sergeant?'

It was almost as if he was daring Peters to open his mouth and load him with any more catastrophes.

Peters cleared his throat unhappily. Whatever he might have hoped to say, Timson was there ahead of him.

'I'll tell you what the problem is, mate. Your blokes seem to have mislaid my prisoner, what I've come all the way down here to clobber the way he ought to be clobbered.'

Thirteen

Conway was in no mood to be obliging, least of all to Frank Burnside. He listened sceptically to the DI's latest appeal for assistance, and his latest assurances that this time they were on to something reliable. If his info was right, then it would be only a matter of hours before they wrapped up the iffy little business of the missing CD players and food mixers.

'Yes,' said Conway glacially. 'If your info is reliable. But how reliable is it, Frank?'

'How long is a bit of string, guv? The point is, I need a body to do the legwork and check it out. I've got Roach and Dashwood up to their necks on another aspect of the job, Greig's tied up in court on a nonce case, and Carver's away on some psychological course. I reckon young Quinnan, say, would suit me down to the ground.'

'Look, Frank, I've just had an ear-bashing about cutting corners and bending the rules, and I'll mark your card here and now that your name was mentioned as chief offender on more than one occasion.'

'Don't tell me. Monroe, right?'

'He's waging a one-man war on station procedure. So if you want Quinnan attached to your team, I think you'd best clear it first with Mr Do-it-by-the-book.'

'Oh, come on, sir, I haven't got time to ponce about. It all started with Quinnan's collar in the first place. He deserves to be in on it.'

Conway let out a weary sigh.

Burnside added: 'I've got a feeling in my water about this one.'

'Me too,' said Conway resignedly.

Burnside emerged triumphant and went off in search of Dave Quinnan. The PC was heading towards the canteen, but came to a halt when Burnside hailed him.

'Right, let's be having you.'

'Sir?'

'You want a piece of the ongoing action, or what? After all, you started it.'

For a moment Quinnan looked baffled, but then the penny dropped. He grinned. 'Too right I do, guvnor.'

'Right, then. Get yourself out of that blue serge and be in my office in five minutes.'

He was satisfied with his choice. Quinnan was the right man for a job like this. He had a hunter's instinct and a disregard for stuffy procedure. As police constables went, PC Quinnan went hard at it.

Burnside drove a circuitous route through the trading estate to come unobtrusively alongside a factory unit. This was the one where Peter the Ponce had sworn there was a lot of hooky gear coming in and going out. With a bit of luck it might prove to be a regular Aladdin's cave – or the home of the Forty Thieves. Either way the result could be magic.

A cold wind was lifting puffs of dust from the road and a long loading bay. Somewhere a loose piece of metal sheeting was clanging a syncopated beat against a wall. A lorry drove out of the yard, and two BMWs drove in. Burnside studied the layout of the roadways and parking spaces, and the doorways in a neighbouring block.

Quinnan, shifting in his seat, was disconcerted by the lull after they had driven here so fast. 'So we just sit and watch, sir?'

'Not we, old son. You.' Burnside slapped a radio against Quinnan's chest. 'Cop for that. Shove it up your jumper, and if anything happens you don't play the big hero, right? You get straight on the wire to me. Don't talk to anyone else but me, understand?'

'Well, yes, sir.' Quinnan opened his door. A draught cut

155

across their ankles. 'What am I supposed to be watching for?'

'Anything that looks a bit sussy or out of the way. Have to use your instinct. That's what I picked you for.' Burnside nodded towards one of the doorways in the nearby block. 'Nice little spot there out of the wind. Have fun. I'll make myself inconspicuous. But you shout, and I'll come running. That's a promise.'

He watched Quinnan stroll selfconsciously across the wide exposed space, and settle himself in the shadow of the doorway. It was up to him what he said if somebody came out unexpectedly. Burnside drove away, off the estate and into the nearest shopping street. There was a vacant thirty-minute parking slot in the slip-road before a line of small shops. He coasted into it, took his time getting out, and went into a tobacconist's to buy a packet of mints and a newspaper. As he returned, his radio crackled into life.

'Message from WPC Marshall. Would you contact on landline. Over.'

This meant urgent business and tricky business. Burnside looked up and down the street for a call-box. There was one close to traffic lights at the end of the row of shops; and an elderly woman was just doddering her way out of it as he reached it. A young man sitting on the edge of a low wall got to his feet and moved towards the box, but Burnside was there first.

The news was, as he might have guessed, not good. The release of Peter the Ponce had begun to set up nasty reverberations. There had been a complaint at the desk, and Inspector Monroe was adding his own complaints. Whatever deal Inspector Burnside might have made, implied Cathy Marshall, he had very little time in which to unmake it. She had stuck her neck out channelling this call outside the main consoles. In return she recommended that Peter the Ponce be rushed in without delay.

Cursing, Burnside went back to the car and retraced the brief route to the trading estate. In his absence some workmen had arrived to set up a canvas hut and unload an armoury of tools. Quinnan, whose contemplation of the suspect unit seemed to have paid no dividends so far, looked round in surprise as the car returned to the kerb. He glanced both ways to make sure he was not observed, and strolled with apparent unconcern across the road.

Burnside wound his window down. 'Where can we lay our hands on the Ponce a bit rapid? I've got to give him back to the system.'

'Was he ever out of the system, then?'

There was no time for lengthy explanations. 'Where does he hang out, do you know?'

'Only seen him a few times till today. Didn't know who he was till Sergeant Peters identified him. But I think I've spotted him this time of day hanging around the amusement arcade. Bit out of order this, though, sir . . . I mean . . .'

'What do you care, old son? I can only play the hand I'm dealt. The governor of the boozer wants to press charges, so it's end of story.' Or maybe, thought Burnside dourly, there might be some unsavoury later instalments not to his own liking.

'What about this gaff? We pack it in?'

Burnside stared yearningly at the uncommunicative front of the factory. It hurt him to think of abandoning the search before it had even properly begun. Bad enough to face being ranted at by a slag like Peter the Ponce for having reneged on their bargain; worse to write the whole thing off without any compensations.

'What wouldn't I give,' he breathed, 'to have a gander inside.'

'Search warrant?'

'What magistrate's going to issue a warrant on the strength of a bubble up from the lowlife? No, we've got to think on our feet. Any ideas?'

'I could go in and make out I'm looking for a job?'

Burnside shook his head. His attention was distracted for a moment by the sudden screech of a drill beginning to attack

157

the road surface fifty yards away. He looked at the group of workmen, two of them languidly unrolling a length of cable from a small drum. He sniffed. 'You smell gas?'

'No.'

'Reckon they might have bust a gas pipe?'

Quinnan cottoned on. 'Oh yeah. Wouldn't be surprised.'

'Go in there and let them know. Think you can handle it?'

'Reckon so. But' – Quinnan's earlier uncertainties surfaced again – 'what will I be looking for, sir?'

'Don't know exactly. Just get inside and keep your eyes open.'

Before turning away, Quinnan said: 'This is all a bit off the record, is it, sir?'

'Yeah, it is. Tell you straight, though, if we had to do everything by the book, we'd never get the job done. Look, if you can't handle it –'

'I can handle it,' said Quinnan cockily. 'Just wanted to know the score.'

He walked off towards the factory unit. The door opened when he was only a few yards away. A man looked him up and down, glancing across at the workmen in the road, and then exchanging a few words. After a minute he reached inside the door and waved to somebody. Quinnan was being provided with a donkey jacket and a hard hat.

Burnside checked his dashboard clock and wondered how long Sun Hill would wait for Peter the Ponce's return before exploding.

Inspector Monroe had two minutes to spare before going to answer a summons from Chief Inspector Conway. Knowing what was likely to be in store, he worked off some of his own anger on the hapless Sergeant Peters with a fusillade of questions about the prisoner who had been so unceremoniously freed from custody.

'With all due respect, sir,' Peters fought back, 'we do know how to pull him again if needed, and as things stood –'

'As things stood, we have someone bringing charges and a uniformed officer who can vouch for what he saw and who he saw . . . and all at once there's nobody there to bring the charges against anyway.'

'On instructions from a superior officer, sir –'

'Whose instructions?'

Peters hesitated. But there was no point in trying to shield someone they both knew to be the guilty party. 'Inspector Burnside did have a long time with him. I had no reason to suspect –'

'If the address that little shyster gave you was a moody one, you've gone and left yourself wide open.'

'If the information Inspector Burnside received checks out, it'll end up in a better result all round.'

'No, Alec, not all round. It just means a better result for CID and Frank Burnside.'

This was too much for Peters. 'I thought we were all on the same side.'

'Don't give me all that.' Monroe gritted his teeth but lowered his voice. 'Look. I realize I've a reputation for doing things by the book. And I'm aware that rules get bent, or massaged, where and when it's deemed necessary to put a villain away. I can live with that. It's a fact of life. But I do not bend rules myself and I'm damned if I'm going to have my own people bending them. Understand what I'm saying, Alec?'

'Yes, sir.'

'Good. I don't care what Frank Burnside and CID get up to. If they want to cut corners, that's down to them. Though we're all hoping,' he said fervently, 'that DCI Wray will have a better influence on dangerous cornering when he gets down to it. In the meantime I don't want Burnside assuming he's entitled to use my people unless it's all up front, by the book and kosher. So in future, Alec, if Inspector Burnside wants a favour, you just send him along to see me. Okay?'

'Yes, sir.'

'Good.' Monroe allowed himself a smile. 'Here endeth the lesson.'

He had lost his smile by the time he reached Conway's office, preparing himself for another lesson.

The handwritten report lay prominently on the chief inspector's desk. Conway had cleared other papers away in order to focus on the offending sheet.

He did not ask Monroe to sit down, but let fly at once. 'I've read this again, Andrew, and my opinion of it has not improved. You're an experienced enough officer to know the golden rule: never put anything down on paper unless you have to.'

'It was on unheaded paper,' Monroe pointed out stiffly, 'unsigned, and there were only three copies. I wrote all three out by hand rather than have any secretary or anyone else get a sniff of it. In view of your reaction, I can assure you that two copies have already gone through the shredder. This one will follow just as soon as you want it to.'

'It can't be too soon.' Conway glowered. 'I tell you, Andrew, it's going to take me some time to forget this.'

'My whole intention was to be helpful. To raise points I honestly felt needed discussion. And put them down in some sort of order instead of sitting in Mr Brownlow's office just talking things over in general and then forgetting half what's been said.'

'I suppose I must accept that. But I won't be in any mood to accept any more of the same kind. Let's leave it at that, shall we?' As Monroe made to leave, Conway said in a more amenable tone: 'Oh, by the way, Inspector Burnside requested the use of one of your people for a few hours at the end of the relief.'

Monroe turned back in the doorway, feigning ignorance. 'Not from me, he didn't.'

'I didn't think you'd have any objection, so I gave him young Quinnan. Good experience for him.'

'This job wouldn't have anything to do with information received, would it?'

160

'Yes, as a matter of fact.' Conway began to look uneasy. 'You know something I don't, Andrew?'

'Only that the DI got a prisoner released in return for that information.'

'Not the first time he's done it, Andrew, and I doubt it'll be the last.'

'Oh, but it will be, sir.'

Conway was jarred by Monroe's aggressiveness; which was exactly what Monroe had intended.

'Andrew, there are times –'

'This is just the sort of thing I included in that report. Just the sort of thing you'd sooner not read about, sir. A perfect illustration, if I may say so.'

'Of what?'

'The original arrest was uniform's. Burnside kicked the man back out on to the street without charge, and in doing so could have dropped one of our own people right in it.'

'Who?'

'Alec Peters. Inspector Burnside is the grand master at using people to break and bend the rules to suit himself. He can do it with his own people, but not with mine.'

'I think you're being a little hard on the man, Andrew.'

'You do, sir? As we speak,' said Monroe with malicious relish, 'two of his own officers are in danger of investigation for interrogating a suspect in the rear of a CID car. No prizes for guessing who instigated that one. And what do you suppose he might be letting Quinnan in for?'

The centre of the factory floor was a maze of cartons stacked on wooden pallets. The foreman led the way round one pile and along an interminable row of shelving. Every now and then he glanced at Dave Quinnan unfavourably, anxious to have this unexpected prowl quickly over and done with.

'No need to evacuate the premises,' Quinnan blithely reassured him. He was almost beginning to believe his own role. 'You don't have any naked flames?'

'No, we haven't.' The man was the type you could rely on

161

to be permanently suspicious of authority. If you asked him about the weather he would find a way of casting doubt on the sky and the Meteorological Office in one breath.

Quinnan spotted a man leaning against a tower of boxes, smoking. 'Excuse me – put that fag out, would you?'

'D'you what?'

Quinnan glanced aside at the foreman. 'As a matter of interest, what kind of business do you run here?'

'What's that got to do with you?'

'Well, you know, just in case.'

The foreman was becoming suspicious. 'A bit casual, ain't ya?'

Two burly men in brown overalls appeared suddenly from behind one of the stacks. Without making any openly aggressive move they were contriving to block Quinnan's way. He looked up at the railed galleries of the upper floor and took a casual step towards an iron staircase. 'Mind if I just check up there?'

As he set foot on the lower tread of the stairs he felt the radio under his jacket begin to slip. He tried to clamp his elbow against it, but it was too late. It fell with a resounding clatter to the floor.

The foreman pounced. 'I thought so! Thought I could smell Old Bill!' He threw the radio aside and swung a vicious punch into Quinnan's stomach. The donkey jacket took some of the force, but not enough to save Quinnan from reeling backwards and thumping into the stair rail. One of the other men kicked his right leg from under him, and kicked again as he went down.

'He won't be alone. Quick, have a gander out front. I'll check the back.'

Quinnan rolled to one side and found his hand near the radio. He hunched up on to his knees and gasped into it: 'Qui . . . Quinnan to Burn . . . Burnside.'

'Drop it!' A boot thudded into Quinnan's shoulder, and another one sent the radio spinning away across the floor.

A voice somewhere was yelling: 'It's all on top – leg it!'

The footsteps pounded away at last. Quinnan pushed himself groggily upright, still unsure that there would not be someone to slam him back down again. But the doors were wide open; there was the roar of a van starting up behind the factory; and he found himself tottering towards the outside world. Light was hurting his right eye, and his lip was burning with agony where it had squashed against one of the metal steps. His right leg did not feel too good, either.

He reached the exit and supported himself for a moment against one of the doors.

Inspector Burnside had shot out of the car and was running towards him. He was halfway across the space in front of the building when a 20-cwt van skidded round the corner and came straight at him. Quinnan, frozen with terror, saw the inspector waver to right, then left, then turn and flee back towards his car. It was parked too close to the end of the driveway. The van tyres screeched, and it swung murderously at the corner and across the kerb. As Burnside leaped to safety, the bonnet of his car was crumpled by a sidelong collision and the offside door went flying several yards down the road. The van backed off to complete its turn, and put the fear of God into the workmen in the middle of the road. Burnside made an attempt to trot after it, then gave up.

Quinnan left the building and made his way to the twisted shape of the car. Burnside joined him, panting. Quinnan felt that when it came to breathing hard and being sympathized with, he deserved priority.

In the morning Burnside arrived early in the CID office to find out what the situation was on all fronts. He was halfway across the yard when he saw Dave Quinnan limping towards the side entrance to the building.

'Hey, how you doing then, son?'

'Morning, sir.' Quinnan touched his swollen lip and winced. 'I'm all right. Just a bit sore, that's all.'

'Well, that's fine then, eh? Play it clever and you'll get ten days off with full pay.' Burnside slapped him on the shoulder, which was not by any means what Quinnan was in the mood for this morning.

Inside, Dashwood and Roach offered a mixed reception. There was some good news, and some not so good news. Half a dozen sets of fingerprints from the factory and three nearly perfect sets from the van, found abandoned by the railway siding, matched up with some familiar ones which the computer was already spitting happily out. The not so good news was that not one set of dabs could be matched to Kenning, the driver of the truck from which the CD players and food mixers had disappeared. It all ought to slot in neatly, but it refused to do so.

'We all know he's dirty,' said Ted Roach, 'but . . .' He shrugged resignedly. When his phone rang he perked up for a moment, hoping against hope for some last-minute revelation. Then he shrugged again, and handed the phone to Burnside.

It was Inspector Monroe. And Monroe, biting off the end of each word, wanted to meet Burnside in the recreation room. It seemed an odd place, but then a lot of odd things went on in Sun Hill. Burnside ambled along to the recreation room, to find Monroe sitting alone at a table. 'Something wrong with your office, old son? Haven't found some cracks in the floorboards already, have we?'

Monroe said: 'I wanted this well away from either of our offices.'

'Going to take long?' Burnside scented trouble, but tried to keep things chatty. 'Only you see, me and mine have a few villains to lift.'

'No, this is not going to take long.' Monroe got up, made sure the door was closed, and stood threateningly in front of the detective inspector. 'Just want a quiet little word in your shell-like, strictly in private.'

'You're learning the lingo,' said Burnside admiringly.

'There's nothing I can learn from you, Burnside. Not a thing.'

'All right, Andrew. Let's try a bit of cooperation, shall we? Say what you feel you've got to say, and let me get on with my work.'

'You are a user and an abuser,' said Monroe. 'You don't give a toss about anyone else's situation just so long as you come out of it covered in results.'

'Oh, grow up, you berk.'

'You had a spawny result, and you know it. And before you go swaggering around here playing Jack the Lad, you just stop and think what the consequences could have been for my people had it all gone pear-shaped on you'.

'Listen, we've all had a result. We've recovered nigh on fifty grand's worth of stolen gear –'

'The result is not the issue here, and you know it. First you dropped Alec Peters right in it, and then you proceed to use another of my people to gain illegal entry into a suspect premises where he ends up on the wrong end of a kicking.'

'Quinnan's all right. I've just spoken to him in the yard.'

'He happens to have come out of it all right, yes. But no thanks to you. You were sat outside in a nice warm car. And some flyer that turned out to be, eh?'

'Now just hold your horses here, old son.'

'No, you listen to me, mister.' Monroe looked as dangerous as the van that had come hurtling towards Burnside yesterday. 'I do not give a fig what you do with your own people, but if you ever set up my blokes again I'll come after you like a bat out of hell. I'll have your head on a pike. Do I make myself clear?'

The two men glared at each other. Burnside fought clear of the eye-wrestling with a forced grin. 'I think you've made your point, Andrew. If you're all done, then . . .?'

'Good. We should chat like this more often. Though,' concluded Monroe with a poisoned parting shot, 'maybe we won't need to when DCI Wray gets back from the snowy slopes.'

It was beneath Burnside's dignity to rise to that one. He opened the door and looked back with a wry nod.

Monroe had obviously been saving something up for the last minute. 'Just one little thing, Frank.' He pulled a small tape recorder from his pocket and held it out across the table. 'Just to let you know you didn't win all the points on this one.'

Burnside studied it with mounting suspicion. Surely the devious sod hadn't been recording their whole conversation? He tried to recall what he had said, and how much of it could be interpreted as sounding incriminating.

Monroe grinned. 'I took this from the stolen batch recovered from that unit yesterday.'

'Tut, tut, now that's against the rules, Andrew. After all you've been saying, an' all! Smack legs.'

'Made under special licence. For export only. Can't purchase them in the UK.'

'That's a riveting bit of info. And now if you don't mind –'

'Your suspect truck driver, Kenning' – Monroe rolled it appreciatively round his taste buds – 'used one identical to this to record a certain conversation in the back of a CID car.'

Burnside could hardly believe his ears. 'You jest?'

'I think you'll find your Mr Kenning has some explaining to do about that coincidence, don't you?'

Burnside nodded gleefully. 'Nice one, Andrew. Nice one.'

'Yes,' said Monroe, now really making a meal of it. 'I thought so, too.'

Fourteen

It had been several weeks since Sun Hill had last had a call from the Alderman Webster Primary School. When one came, it sounded the usual thing. There had been a break-in. Only this time, just for a change, the school video and computer had not been lifted.

'And no food mixers?' said Dave Quinnan, nursing the memory of his last encounter with such items.

'I don't think they mix food on school premises nowadays,' said Sergeant Penny. 'Isn't it just delivered in containers and re-heated?'

'Haven't got any kids. I wouldn't know.'

'All the same, you're the expert on that sort of thing. Just nip along and see if you can add a black eye to your purple lip.'

Quinnan went off in a panda. It was a nice restful way of passing the odd hour or so at the beginning of a morning.

The sound of ragged singing poured out of an open window as he crossed the playground. Whatever the hymn might have been, it was not one which Quinnan had chanted during his schooldays; or else someone had found a weird way of disguising it.

There was barely a pause between the last notes and the opening of the hall door. Quinnan flattened himself against the corridor wall as children marched out and then split up into different streams, racing and stumbling off to various classrooms. One or two looked eagerly at the uniformed PC, obviously hoping that something gory had happened on the premises. During a gap in the unruly procession, he dodged across the corridor and into the secretary's office.

167

The secretary was a fussy middle-aged woman who first complained about the length of time he had taken to get here, and then made it clear that the headmaster would be conferring a great favour by seeing him. She led the way through to an inner room, calling, 'There's a constable here at last.'

Mr Thorpe was in his early forties, with a pointed beard which probably disguised a weak chin, and looked so harassed that you doubted his chances of making fifty. He muttered thanks to the secretary, held out a nervous hand to Quinnan, and then ushered him immediately out of the office again.

'Visited again last night,' he said fretfully. 'I'll show you where they got in.'

'Anything missing?'

'Not this time. They were probably after the video and computer again, but since we followed your advice last time this place is getting like Fort Knox. What it's cost means we've had to give up buying books. But nobody cares about books nowadays, anyway.'

They crossed a central display area with posters and artwork on the walls. All of them seemed connected with animals, and as Quinnan skirted a table he looked down into a glass case containing something with more legs and antennae than seemed natural. He wondered queasily what went on in the school laboratory.

'It's Animal Week,' Thorpe explained. 'We're caring about the world's fauna. From giant pandas to stick insects.'

They went through a side door into the extreme end of the hall, below the platform. Evidently not all the morning's assembly had made a rush out through the main exit. Two groups of eight-year-olds sat on the floor, arms locked round their knees, staring gravely up at a man with an amiable but lined face, his greying hair straggling around a wide bald patch like a monk's tonsure. A girl teacher sat on a plastic-backed hall chair, smiling at the children every now and then, and smiling at the man. He had the sort of endearing, shy expression which automatically evoked an answering smile.

'Hands up all those who've got a dog.'

As they made a circuit round the children, Quinnan noticed that a large soft toy dog dressed in a red jacket was propped on another chair alongside the girl teacher.

'Sorry, Mr Blake,' said the headmaster, heading for the opposite door.

'Not at all.' Blake's voice had a deferential smile in it, too. 'Now children. Hands up those who haven't got a dog but have got some other kind of pet.'

Hands waved in the air.

'Yes, lovey.' Blake pointed to one of the more agitated little girls. 'What have you got?'

As they emerged on to a path which led into a shaded corner of the buildings, Quinnan was aware of some unformed, misty doubt drifting across the back of his mind. There was no shape or substance to it, yet somehow he was uneasy.

'That dog on the staff, is he?' Even the thought of the friendly atmosphere in there made him grin instinctively.

'No, that's Mervyn the Mongrel. Mr Blake's mascot.'

'Mr Blake's one of your teachers, then?'

'No, he just comes in once a year to talk to the children. Does a lot for "Dogs in Danger", an animal welfare charity. Been doing it for years.' Thorpe stopped by a window with a large blank gap where glass ought to have been. Someone had sawn away neatly at the bottom and one edge, but must then have been clumsy, letting the large pane fall away and smash on to the floor of the room within. 'We've left everything as found,' said Thorpe self-importantly. 'I had the door of the room locked at once so that nobody would get in.'

'Does he visit all the local schools, then?'

Thorpe blinked. 'Sorry?'

'Mervyn the Mongrel,' said Quinnan.

'Really, officer, I think that with important matters on hand that's a trifle frivolous . . .'

Quinnan tried to keep his attention on Thorpe's important

169

matters, made a few routine notes, and wrapped it all up as quickly as possible so that he could hurry back to Sun Hill.

He was striding towards the murder incident room when Sergeant Penny intercepted him.

'You been to the school?'

'Yes, sarge. Nothing stolen. NFA, I should think, once the SOCO'S had a look.'

'Sorry if it was boring for you,' said Penny with heavy sarcasm. 'I've had a fun time as well, checking your corres bin. Would now be a good moment to discuss warrants?'

'Not really, sarge, I need a leak.'

'Front office, five minutes.'

'Yes, sergeant.'

Quinnan continued on his way to the incident room. The action board was still on the wall and the action book still on the table, but a large number of chairs had been removed and there were now only two telephones. Computer printouts were stacked in one corner. Alastair Greig was taking a phone call without enthusiasm. The room was operating now on a skeleton staff. The work was boring, the information slowing to a trickle; and most of that was irrelevant rubbish.

'A group of travellers,' Greig repeated wearily. 'Yeh. Thank you, sir. Twenty-second of last month?'

Quinnan pointed to the stack of files on shelving beside the action board, his eyebrows asking permission to check something out. Greig waved indifferently. Quinnan snapped back the clip of the top file, but its contents consisted mainly of the most recent statements from what could only loosely be called witnesses. So few people had actually witnessed anything at all – which did not stop them coming in or phoning in with incredibly circumstantial tales. He ducked to lift out an older box, going back to the original discovery of Jennie Price's body. Here there was a bundle of statements which had been written off as even less dependable than those provided by later testifiers. The incoherent ramblings of the Gilfillan Street winos could never

170

have been seriously expected to provide any hard, useful evidence.

Quinnan leaned on the cabinet, jotting down the key factors in his notebook. Greig, curious, was just about to cut short the phone conversation and come across to see what was going on when Quinnan pushed the bundle back into the drawer, waved his thanks, and hurried off to use the front office phone. If his hunch was wrong, he did not want to be made a laughing-stock and have snide remarks wafting about for the next few months. If he was right, he wanted to be quite sure before claiming the credit and setting the wheels in motion.

Norse Hill Primary School confirmed what he had suspected. Taking a deep breath, he tried St Eunice's. They kept him waiting a few minutes, and out of the corner of his eye he saw Sergeant Penny resolutely approaching. Then they came up with it.

'Yes, that was it. You're quite right: the thirtieth of April. But why? Is there something –'

'Just routine,' said Quinnan reassuringly. 'Thanks for your help.'

'Quinnan . . .'

'Be right back, sarge.'

He headed past the incident room and knocked on the door of the adjoining office. There was no reply. When he opened the door and looked in, the room was empty.

At his elbow Ted Roach said: 'Who are you after?'

'AMIP. Superintendent Meadows.'

'Not here today. Not here most days, come to that.'

'Who's top man on the murder enquiry, then?'

Roach shrugged. 'The guvnor. Our Mr Wray's in the chair now, refreshed from his vacation and ready to get his teeth into whatever's juicy. If anything *is*.' Roach had been the most vociferous in vowing to follow up the murder of those two children, no matter how long it took; but hope had grown dimmer, other work had taken priority, and now the heat was off. He showed no sign of believing that there could be a sudden resurgence. 'What's it about?'

'Can we find Mr Wray?' Dave Quinnan had no intention of handing it all over direct to Ted Roach.

Equally, Roach had no intention of letting a mere PC confide things to a senior CID officer without him being in on it. He accompanied Quinnan to Wray's office and stood to one side, making it clear that he had been part of this operation from the start and was still part of it.

DCI Gordon Wray was ready to listen, though at first his bleak stare was not meant to encourage the theories of an over-eager uniformed officer.

Quinnan kept it formal, simply reciting the facts and letting them speak for themselves.

He told of visiting the Alderman Webster School on a routine inquiry into a break-in, and of seeing Donald Blake there. At the time he had not known the man's Christian name, but during his phone conversations with two other schools he had learnt it. Blake visited most primary schools in the area from time to time and talked to the children about an animal charity he was connected with. Everywhere he went he took a mascot: a big toy dog, dressed in red. Seeing the dog had rung the bell for Quinnan. There was some connection with the Jennie Price murder. Having dug out the witness statements, he found confirmation. One of the Gilfillan Road winos had claimed to have seen a big dog in a red coat driving a car.

'He was the one,' Roach interjected, 'who later claimed it was a black panther driving a red bus. He was the most spaced out of the lot. And the smelliest.'

Quinnan kept his eyes on Wray. 'But I think he was right the first time, sir. Donald Blake visited the schools of both murder victims during the relevant period.' He flipped back a page of his notebook. 'He was at Norse Hill Primary, Graeme Butler's school, on the eighth of February. And St Eunice's C of E on the thirtieth of April – the day before Jennie Price was murdered.'

172

Wray's set expression did not alter, but he leaned forward and said quietly, almost respectfully: 'And do you have Mr Blake's address?'

'Yes, sir.'

The three of them went along the corridor together. In the front office they separated. Enviously Quinnan watched Wray and Roach going together out of the front door. That was where he ought to have been – with them, instead of waiting here for the wrath of Sergeant Penny to fall around his ears.

'I don't know why you're playing so hard to get, Quinnan. I'm not after your body.' Penny waved a sheaf of warrants. 'Just an explanation of why these haven't been executed.'

'Sorry, sergeant.' Quinnan admired his own coolness. 'I just thought solving a murder might be more important.'

The house was a post-war semi-detached villa in a quiet suburban street. A wrought iron gate led through a well-tended privet hedge on to a path completely devoid of weeds or straying grass. When Wray rang the doorbell, the front door was opened by a homely-looking woman with a closely cropped, no-nonsense hairdo. She wore a plain blue skirt, spotless white cardigan, and a blue blouse buttoned up to the neck. Her smile was polite but unencouraging. She appeared the kind of housewife who was used to salesmen coming to the door, and used to turning them civilly away.

'Good morning, madam. Detective Chief Inspector Wray and Detective Sergeant Roach, Sun Hill police. We were hoping to speak to Mr Donald Blake.'

'Why, whatever's the matter?'

Wray took it very correctly, step by step. 'Mrs Blake?'

'Yes.'

'Is your husband at home, please?'

'No, I'm afraid he's not.'

'Could you tell us when he's likely to be back?'

'About tea-time, I expect.'

'Perhaps you could spare us a few minutes instead, then. Would that be possible, Mrs Blake?'

She looked bewildered, not accustomed to having the police standing on her doorstep. Unsure how best to cope, she stood aside. Wray and Roach stepped in. The hall was exactly what you would have expected from the outside, with gleamingly polished banisters rising from the thickly carpeted floor to the upper landing, and a mat placed immediately inside the door for wiping one's feet. A blue vase garnished with artificial flowers stood in the narrow window at the bottom of the stairs. There were three prints of animal drawings on one wall.

The living-room into which Mrs Blake showed them was equally predictable. The loose covers of the three-piece suite matched the flowered curtains; the television was set at an angle in one corner with the settee facing it squarely; and two public library books were placed neatly on a glass-topped table, their spines lined up exactly along its gilded rim. It was suburban, comfortable, and like a thousand other such rooms except for one conspicuous feature. Sprawled in an armchair was a large toy dog in a red coat.

Roach eyed it with a dawning sense that the guesses were all about to come true, the whole thing really was going to add up. 'This must be Mervyn.'

Mrs Blake laughed nervously. 'Well, yes. Fancy you –'

'Your husband's obviously been back from Alderman Webster's, then? said Wray.

'Yes, you've only missed him by about ten minutes.'

'Would you know where he's gone?'

'I've honestly no idea. It's his day off. If it's dry he takes a packed lunch and the one that barks, and off he goes.'

'I'm sorry?' Wray had sat down without being invited but with an assumption of friendliness that nobody could take amiss. 'The one that barks?'

Mrs Blake was relaxing, lulled by the easy-going approach. 'We've got two dogs, Mervyn and a real one. A Border collie. Her name's Sal but she always gets called "the one that barks".'

'Border collie,' mused Roach: 'black and white?'

174

'Yes.' Mrs Blake's brief interlude of relaxation was being undermined. 'Why? What's wrong? Why do you need to see Donald?'

Roach left it to his DCI to tackle the next bit, where it could get really painful. That was what promotion lumbered you with.

Wray was dodging it, postponing it for a few moments. 'Could you tell us what your husband was wearing when he went out, Mrs Blake?'

She answered automatically, too bewildered to protest. 'Grey trousers and his old fawny-coloured shirt, I think. Oh, and his green pullover. What he always wears.'

'And he took his car?'

'Yes.'

Roach opened his notebook. 'And that would be a dark blue Maestro, registration F436 RND?'

'Yes.' Mrs Blake latched on to this. 'It's the car, then? Is he in trouble over it? I keep nagging him about that headlamp.'

'There's no problem with the car as far as we know, Mrs Blake.'

'Then what? What are you here for?'

Roach kept very still. Wray said: 'Basically just trying to clear up a long-standing inquiry. Your husband's one of the people we'd like to eliminate if we can. Nothing to get alarmed about. In fact, if you could confirm his whereabouts on two particular dates, that would more or less be the end of it.'

'Does your husband keep a diary?' asked Roach casually.

Mrs Blake shook her head. 'He puts things on the kitchen calendar, that's all.'

'Would it be possible to see the calendar?'

As if in a trance she shuffled out, unsure of her footing in her own house.

'I hope it's not him,' muttered Roach. 'It'll kill her.'

Wray made no response but waited, motionless, until Mrs Blake came back with a wall calendar adorned with colour

175

photographs of pretty kittens. She watched Wray working his way methodically down each leaf, until she could bear the silence no longer.

'Would you like a cup of tea?'

'No thanks, love.' It was Roach who took it on himself to reply. 'We'll be gone soon.'

Mrs Blake stared again at Wray and at the calendar in his hands. 'Does it help?'

'Not really.' Wray turned the sheet towards her. 'Sunday the fifteenth here. Would your husband have taken Sal for a walk that evening?'

'Possibly.'

He turned a couple of pages. 'And this Tuesday here, the first? In the morning?'

'Most Tuesdays he goes to Wimbledon.'

'Work?'

'He's a wages clerk for Metcalf and Pryor. He travels round the firm's different factories.'

'By car?'

'Yes.'

'Does he ever take Sal to work with him?'

'Occasionally. If he's going to finish early, and there's somewhere nice for her to run.'

'So she could have been with him on this particular Tuesday morning, could she – when he was going to Wimbledon?'

'It's possible, yes. I honestly don't know. I go out before him on Tuesdays. I have a little job at the Health Centre.'

'And you've no idea where he might be now?'

'No, I've told you.' She was becoming more and more distressed, not having the faintest idea where all this was leading. 'I'm not a great one for walking. That's why he takes the dog. For company. Look, what is it, this inquiry you want to eliminate Donald from?'

Roach was almost as much on edge as she was. He was tired of Wray's evasiveness and the would-be polite line that

176

the DCI thought so clever-clever. It was time to come out with it and let her know what she was facing.

'It's a murder inquiry, Mrs Blake,' he said bluntly. 'The deaths of Graeme Butler and Jennie Price. I'm sure you must have heard about them.'

Stunned, she looked from one man to the other.

With a glare at Roach, Wray tried to keep up his blandly reassuring tone. 'Mrs Blake, we interview hundreds of innocent people in the course of such an inquiry. Anyone we feel can help us in any way. We now feel your husband may be able to help us, and we'd be failing in our duty if we didn't speak to him.'

'But why?' Her nice, ordinary, homely face was ravaged by an uncomprehending terror. 'Whatever makes you think –'

'It's not what we think. I must stress that. Almost certainly it's a matter of coincidence, but that's our job, checking such things.'

'What coincidence?' When he did not answer, she went on, distraught: 'But it's just not possible. He loves children. We've got a grandson of our own. He means the world to Donald.'

'I'm sure that's so, which is why we're anxious to clear this up as quickly as possible.' Wray stretched his legs, looking very much at home in the Blakes' living-room. 'I appreciate this isn't very pleasant for you. I can only say again that your husband is just someone we'd like to speak to: that's all.'

'Then find him,' Mrs Blake burst out suddenly. She looked on the verge of tears, but controlled herself with an effort. 'I don't know how you can come here and say such things. Now go away. Please go away.'

Roach looked at Wray, willing him not to push it any further. Wray gave a slight nod, and got up.

'I'm sorry, Mrs Blake. Thank you for your time. If your husband should come home before we . . . before we make contact with him, I'd be grateful if he could phone us at Sun Hill.'

She was beyond speech. When they left the room she

did not follow, but left them to open the front door and let themselves out.

As Wray opened the car door, Roach ventured: 'Should we send Viv to sit with her?'

'Makes it look as if we've already made up our minds, doesn't it?' But Wray nodded. 'She'd better bring in Mervyn the Mongrel as well. Evidence.'

Roach slid into his seat. 'It might still not be him, you know. The number of times we've been wrong on this patch . . .'

'Let's just find him, Ted, eh? He could be at it again this very minute.' Wray reached for the radio. 'Sierra Oscar from Chief Inspector Wray, receiving, over . . .? This is a general call. Wanted urgently for questioning. Donald Blake, white, early fifties, medium height, thinning hair, grey. Wearing grey trousers, fawn-coloured shirt, probably a green pullover. Possibly driving a dark blue Maestro, registration Foxtrot 436 Romeo November Delta. May otherwise be walking a dog in parkland or open space. The dog is a Border collie, black and white. Please notify any sighting immediately.'

Chief Inspector Conway and Inspector Munroe headed briskly towards the CAD room. The whole place was alive, tingling with activity again.

Now, at last, this time . . .

'I want every available body out on patrol, Andrew,' said Conway. 'If this man's on our ground I want him found before the schools turn out.'

'Doesn't give us long, sir.'

'Three and a half hours.'

'Except for Alderman Webster's, sir. They're on a half day. Twelve-thirty finish.'

Conway was shaken. This was a bit of local information he had not caught up with. 'Put a man on the school gate.'

'Right, sir. Though if it is Blake,' observed Monroe, 'he'd be very rash to strike the same day as when he's been visiting, surely?'

178

'Jennie Price was the day immediately after a visit, wasn't she? That was pretty rash, too.' Conway's gaze raked the wall map. 'What's the geography?'

'Alderman Webster's' – Monroe pointed it out in the lower left-hand corner – 'in Fairbrother Road. Pretty dense housing and commercial, but there's open ground in the catchment area. Nearest patch to the school is Whippingham Park.'

'Have it watched. By a reliable officer.'

They swung into action. The hunt was on again, and their appetite was fiercely sharpened by the prospect of a kill.

It was not AMIP now, but Sun Hill. There was no argument about overtime, or duty rosters, or knocking-off time for this relief or any other relief. Peters settled himself at a console, wide awake and prepared to stay that way for as many hours as it took. By remote control he could feel himself moving out over Canley Fields, which Jimmy Carver and Roach were circling; and with Loxton and Datta down towards the Gilfillan Road waste ground, checking for a blue Maestro, unlikely as a killer's return to that grim site might seem; and with Quinnan, out on foot to cover every improbable stretch of grassy verge, back alley and canal path within a tight radius of the Blakes' house.

Behind Peters' head, Conway was saying: 'Don't suppose Wray asked the wife if Blake's ever been to Bristol? They've got two unsolved child murders on their books.'

'Metcalf and Pryor do have a factory down there, sir,' said Monroe, 'at Avonmouth.'

The radios chattered to and fro, reporting in; reporting nothing.

Until Sergeant Tom Penny, getting out of his car at the southern gate to Whippingham Park, leaned on the railings and stared with no great optimism across the grass. A few kids were on the swings, and a little girl was viewing the slide apprehensively, daring herself to climb up and slither down. The backdrop of high-rise blocks cast a heavy shadow across the far corner. A couple of young women pushed prams towards the exit nearest the shopping precinct. One or two elderly people were allowing themselves to be bullied by constant barking into throwing sticks for their dogs. On his own, not mixing with the others, a man with grey hair was throwing a ball for a black and white Border collie. Penny studied him for a long, calculating minute, then leaned towards his radio.

'Sierra Oscar from 54 . . . I think I've found him.'

Inspector Monroe's voice answered incisively. 'Keep tabs on him, Tom. We'll send reinforcements.'

Penny moved cautiously through the gate, afraid of it squeaking as it closed. He must not frighten their quarry away. Yet was there any reason why the man should take fright? He was not to know what had been brewing up while his back was turned. He looked too mild and woolly to take sudden alarm and do a runner.

The ball trundled across the grass again, and the dog went happily after it. Its owner watched indulgently, and stooped to accept the ball as the collie came bounding back. Penny strolled towards the two of them in a long arc, not attempting to hide in those exposed surroundings, but making the approach a very leisurely one. The man did not notice him until he was right on top of them. The dog frisked up, sniffed at Penny's trousers, and frolicked off again.

'Excuse me, sir. Mr Blake?'

'Yes?' Blake seemed quite calm, almost as though he had been expecting this arrival.

'Could you spare a few minutes, sir? We need to speak to you.'

Blake stared unflinchingly at Penny. 'Is it about Graeme and Jennie?'

'Yes, sir. It is.'

Penny was alert now for the man to run away; to make a dash for it, now that he knew. But Blake stayed where he was, and when he reached out his right hand it was not to knock Penny aside but to squeeze his arm very lightly.

'Thank you.'

180

Fifteen

They were virtually queueing up to make brief inspections of Donald Blake through the wicket of his cell door. Sitting on the bench and sipping a cup of tea, thoughtful but calm, he was a bit of a disappointment. Was this what a callous murderer looked like? While Stringer was taking a look, Blake reached absently for a sandwich from the packet lying on the bench beside him. He might almost have been planning a lecture in his head, ready for his next visit to one of the local schools.

'Come on, out of it.' Sergeant Bob Cryer began hustling them away. 'It's not a peepshow.'

As the cell corridor cleared, a grim-faced Ted Roach appeared at the end of it. 'Can we have Mr Blake now, please, Bob.'

Heads turned surreptitiously as the man was led out. There had been a burst of spontaneous applause as Sergeant Tom Penny walked through, with a 'Nice one, sarge,' and a 'Well done, Tom' – warmer approval than the dour Penny was accustomed to – but now there was silence. It seemed incredible that this unassuming little bloke could be a bestial killer, and almost as incredible that he should meekly have surrendered and allowed himself to be brought back to Sun Hill. The two aspects did not seem to go together. Maybe they didn't; maybe, somewhere, there was a mistake and they would be back to square one.

DI Burnside was waiting at the door of the interview room. As Roach led Blake in, he tried to follow, to find his way blocked by DCI Wray.

'Three's a crowd, Frank. It's called oppression.'

'But I could handle this, sir. You've already gone beyond the call of duty, knocking on his door. A DCI –'

'Thank you, Frank. I'll call you when I need you.'

Wray went into the interview room and closed the door. Roach set the tape recorder going, announced the time and date and the names of those present, and Wray settled himself opposite Blake and started. He foresaw no problems. There was no need now for subtle tactics: just say what had to be said, record the answers, and make the charge stick.

'Now, Mr Blake, my understanding is that you were very cooperative when first approached by Sergeant Penny. You came voluntarily to this station, and on the way you confessed willingly to these offences. Is that correct?'

Blake showed no signs of defiance, but neither did he seem interested in what Wray had said or was likely to say. He considered the table. It was impossible to tell what he was thinking: absurdly, he might have been sizing it up as a possible prop for one of his talks – maybe a place on which to sit Mervyn the Mongrel.

'Mr Blake?' Wray prompted quietly.

'I don't want to talk.'

This was not what Wray had expected. 'Why's that? Mr Blake . . .?'

'Because it's none of your business.' Blake was still neither defensive nor pugnacious. He was simply stating what to him was a self-evident fact.

'You told the custody officer you didn't want a solicitor. Have you changed your mind?'

'No.'

'So what's the problem?'

'I can't say these things.' Blake looked up, glancing from Wray to Roach. 'Not to you.' He paused, then said reflectively: 'I'll talk to the sergeant. That's all.'

Roach silently consulted Wray. From Blake's withdrawn expression it was pretty clear that they had no alternative. Wray nodded to Roach to log details of a brief suspension of the interview and switch off the recorder, while he went out of the room.

Burnside was still loitering in the corridor, his face dark with frustration.

'Fetch Tom Penny, please, Frank. Blake wants him to do the interview.'

Burnside's features grew darker. 'No way. Uniform do not interrogate murder suspects.'

'We need him to cough. Officially. The quicker the better, yes?'

'But they're already taking the glory. It's us who's done all the donkey work these past months.'

'He kills children,' said Wray flatly. 'What does it matter who gets him to say it?'

'There are limits, sir. And Tom Penny's beyond mine.'

'Fetch him. Now.'

Sergeant Penny was fetched, and Wray opened the door to the interview room. He nodded to Roach to operate the recorder and keep an eye on things, and backed out. If it was going to work, he sensed it would do so only with the minimum of congestion in that room.

Tom Penny had never had to cope with a procedure of this kind before. Giving routine warnings to suspects pulled in before him in the custody area and tackling them if they got rough was one thing; delicately manoeuvring for the confidence of a man who might, for all they knew, explode into a berserk rage was quite another. The likes of DCI Wray were trained to carry on an interrogation with a calm professional veneer, unmoved by whatever outpourings they might provoke. Penny was torn between disgust and a feeling of incompetence.

He ventured: 'When we met in the park this morning, Donald, what were your . . . um . . . plans for the day?'

'I was there to do it again,' said Blake simply. 'I wanted to do it again.'

'Do what again, Donald?'

183

'Take a child.' Blake looked sideways at Roach, and faltered for a moment. Then he went on more firmly. 'I know it's wrong. That's part of the reason why I do it. Because it's wrong. Because it's beyond anything normal people do. And I've always been very normal. That's what's made it exciting, partly. My secret thing that nobody would dream of. That's very exciting.' He was beaming, almost inviting their approval and understanding. 'Even what I feel about myself afterwards, hating myself for having done it – that's exciting too, in a funny sort of way. So I could never stop myself, you see . . . Tom. Having started, there was no way I could call a halt. But I did want to be stopped. And you stopped me.' Again he was smiling. 'It seems a sort of personal thing between you and me.'

Penny tried to answer in the same remote, unflurried way. 'Did you kill Graeme Butler, Donald?' When Blake merely nodded, he said: 'Does that mean yes?'

'Yes.'

Roach glanced thankfully at the tape recorder.

'And did you also kill Jennie Price?' asked Penny.

'I did, yes.'

Now it came out in a rush. Blake had been bottling it up for so long, but now he wanted to talk. He hardly needed an occasional question to keep him going.

It sounded so straightforward and rational. Donald Blake had always been very fond of children, and of animals. He considered himself a bit sentimental, but was not ashamed of it. He had liked touching them – kids and animals – and having a bit of a cuddle. His wife, Kath, had thought it was soppy, though in her own way she was fond enough of children. She spoilt their grandson whenever she got the chance. But it wasn't the same. She just didn't feel things the same way he did.

'There's sex in it,' Blake admitted reflectively. 'How I feel, I mean. I don't deny that.'

Not that there had always been this sexual element; not when he was younger, so far as he could remember. He had
184

only gradually begun to realize, during his school visits, what effect children of a certain age were having on him. Inside, there were exciting sensations. He felt nervous after he had stroked them, but often they didn't notice, or took it for granted. Then it got worse, and he began to feel ashamed but, as he had said, that was part of it too – the intoxication of being ashamed.

'What happened with Graeme?' asked Penny quietly.

Graeme had been an accident, at any rate to start with. Blake had been out walking Sal, and bumped into the boy. It was nearly dark, and the kid ought really not to have been out on his own. Blake had told him as much. But he got the impression that Graeme was not too happy at home. He was certainly upset about something, so Blake talked to him, and put his arm round him; and one thing led to another until the boy suddenly got frightened. He began shouting and calling Blake names. 'Really bad language,' said Blake disapprovingly. They were near some houses, and the last thing he wanted was for people to get the wrong idea, so he started pulling Graeme away. There was no question of letting the boy go home while he was in such a state.

That was how they had ended up on Cranley Fields.

Looking back, Blake confessed that he was beginning to doubt if it had just been panic. Deep down he had wanted to be with the boy, in the trees. Then Graeme got more and more hysterical, and Blake had to hold on to him more and more tightly. And the tighter he held on, the harder he squeezed, the more wonderful he felt inside. Better and better and better . . .

And then Graeme was dead.

Roach mopped his brow. Penny saw that Roach was sharing his own feelings: horror and loathing, and a desire to strangle this creature right here, in this room, right here and now. Yet at the same time he was such a pathetic little runt. You would still have said, even after hearing all this, that there was no harm in him.

185

Tom Penny held back the nausea in his throat. 'And Jennie Price?'

Viv Martella hesitated on the step of the Blakes' home, then forced herself to ring the bell. Mrs Blake, answering the door, was about to make some dismissive remark and close it again when Martella produced her warrant card.

'Mrs Blake? WDC Martella, Sun Hill police. Just to let you know we've found your husband. He's fine. He's at the station now, sorting things out.' It was like talking into a void. Like sending out a radio message only to realize that the transmission was not being received at the other end. She tried again. 'Mr Wray thought it would be a good idea if someone was with you. You know, company while you're waiting.'

Waiting for what? The woman's set expression suggested that she already knew what the answer would be, even while refusing to believe it was possible.

Before Martella could make another attempt, Mrs Blake turned and went back along the passage, leaving the front door open. Martella stepped in, closing it softly behind her. Between one inner door and another, Mrs Blake said: 'I'll get some tea.'

It was a good idea to leave her to it. Martella waited what seemed an eternity for the tray to arrive, and for Mrs Blake to put little lace doylies quite superfluously on the glass surface of the table. Methodically she poured; methodically set the cups and saucers down; separated two small plates from below a plate of biscuits; and then sat down.

They sipped tea for a while in silence.

'I'm sure it won't take long to check it all out,' said Martella.

Mrs Blake did not even deign to answer. After a few minutes she went to switch the television on, and the two of them blankly watched the end of a golf tournament somewhere far away. When it gave way to a nature programme about
186

dogs in the wild, Mrs Blake gasped faintly and hurried to switch it off.

The phone in the hall began to ring.

Martella put down her cup and saucer, and got up before Mrs Blake could make a move. 'I expect that's for me.'

It was. Roach had sent out some interim news, and Wray said what it was. Could she cope with Mrs Blake?

'Yes. But how much should I . . .'

'Not much point in pretending any longer. You'll have to judge it where you are, on the spot, Viv. But don't let her do anything silly.'

Martella replaced the receiver and went back into the sitting-room. Mrs Blake glanced up, and their eyes met. There was no need to decide how much or how little to tell her. She knew by now.

'I'm sure it'd be all right for you to see your husband,' said Martella. 'By the time we've driven to the station, he should be –'

'No,' she whispered. There was a long silence before she said hoarsely: 'What about Sal?'

Martella was momentarily puzzled. Then she remembered. 'Oh, the dog. She'll be fine. We've got kennels.'

'Can I . . . bring her home?'

'What, now?'

Mrs Blake nodded; and then at last broke into wrenching, uncontrollable tears.

Blake's manner was becoming almost dreamy as he dug back into memories of everything that had come about – memories which still had an appetizing tang like none other.

He had not consciously gone looking for Jennie Price, he reminisced; or, indeed, anyone. But he knew that he wanted it to happen. 'Because when you've had that feeling once, Tom . . . well . . . only I didn't know when, or where.' Then there she was, in Hemsworth Road. Blake did not know her name, any more than he had known Graeme's. He recognized her as a girl from one of the schools he

187

visited, but did not know her name until he read it in the paper afterwards.

That morning he had been driving along Hemsworth Road with what he called his full team: Mervyn in front, and Sal in the back. He had forgotten to take Mervyn indoors the night before. Perhaps if Mervyn had not been there, nothing would have happened. But Jennie saw him, and waved. Blake stopped the car, at first just to say hello. Then Jennie saw the real dog on the back seat, and Sal jumped out, and she and the girl made a fuss of each other.

'You'll have to lift her back in, or I'll be here all day,' Blake had laughed. 'She won't get in on her own.'

Jennie obliged. And once she was inside, still holding Sal, Blake leaned over and shut the door. When Jennie looked startled, he promised to drop her off at school. Instead he took her home. The sheer risk of that was exhilarating. His wife was out doing one of her mornings down at the Health Centre, but there might always be somebody looking, somebody hearing if the girl screamed. He drove straight into the garage, and before she could cry out or get out of the car he had closed the doors.

'And it was just as good,' he told Penny earnestly. 'Afterwards I felt brave ... strong ... like I could walk through a brick wall. So dumping her body was no problem.' He sat back, and sighed at what was gone forever. Without warning he reached forward and squeezed Penny's hand, just as he had squeezed his arm when they met in the park. 'I appreciate you helping me through this, Tom.'

Penny tried not to flinch. Things had been building up inside him, but he could not allow himself to let them out the way Blake had been doing. Not that they would ever, in his worst imaginings, have been as foul as this. His own marriage was childless, his wife was cold and cantankerous and squirmed away from being touched – though she herself told all her friends that of course *he* was the cold and unloving one – and several of Blake's remarks had touched a nerve he hadn't known he possessed. But a confession of vulnerability,

188

which Blake had been wallowing in, was beyond Tom Penny after all these years. He had become an expert in throttling things down.

He was not going to admit that he hated being touched. Only that he hated being touched by a pervert like this: but who wouldn't?

After a moment Blake withdrew his hand. 'I was in Bristol last week.' He came out with it in an abstracted way, as if it were of no immediate consequence. 'Can I tell you about that?'

Chief Superintendent Brownlow's conference room was remarkably quiet, considering the number of officers packed into it. Conway, Wray, Burnside, Monroe and two AMIP detectives had assembled here, waiting for news. When they spoke, it was aimlessly, in fragments. Until the news came, speculation was a waste of time. There was a now-or-never feeling in the air.

When Roach appeared in the doorway there was a moment of absolute silence.

'He's coughed, sir.'

There was a resounding cheer. A beaming Brownlow shook Wray's hand in congratulation. Burnside turned away and looked out of the window.

Brownlow waved expansively at Roach. 'Tell the incident room it's open house up here this afternoon, Ted. I think we'll allow ourselves a little celebration.'

Within a matter of minutes it had all the appearance of a Christmas party. Sun Hill officers in uniform and plain clothes squeezed in to grab a can of beer or a glass of whisky. Brownlow made vaguely appreciative noises in all directions; then became aware that an essential component was missing.

'Where's Tom Penny?'

'Just wrapping it up with Blake, sir. Said he'd been asked to stay there, just for a few minutes – see him to the cell, and everything.'

'While CID drink my whisky? That's uncharacteristically noble of him.'

After making sure that everybody was holding a glass and that the party was in full swing and in no need of his surveillance, Brownlow went next door into his office to make a few phone calls. There would be a press conference at three o'clock that afternoon. Perhaps that would be short notice for some of the senior AMIP officers, but if they failed to turn up then Sun Hill would manage very happily without them. This had been a local triumph, after all. It would be nice to capitalize on the PR, putting a few Sun Hill names and faces in front of the media for a change. Sergeant Penny, for instance, who had arrested the man. And then there was Quinnan. They must both be warned to prepare themselves.

As he returned and found Conway standing slightly back from the main throng, it occurred to him that some other colourful tribute might be in order.

'Derek, we really ought to be thinking about a commendation for somebody.' He beckoned Monroe to join them. 'Andrew, I've just been saying to Derek that I'd be justified in putting forward a name for a commendation. What do you think – Penny or Quinnan?'

Some of the uniformed officers were drifting back to their duties, pausing on the way out for a brisk word of thanks to the chief super. He stopped Bob Cryer in his tracks.

'Bob, let's hear what you think.'

'Sir?'

Brownlow glanced back at Monroe. 'Sorry, Andrew. Go ahead.'

'Well, sir, Sergeant Penny did make the arrest.'

'Yes, indeed.'

'With respect, sir,' Conway broke in, 'I'm not sure that that will wash up the road. He just happened to be there, and the man came quietly. Basically a straightforward collar even in the special circumstances.'

Brownlow turned to Cryer. 'What do you think, Bob?'